DARK WEBS

A Novella of Leda and Helen of Sparta

Debra J. Giuffrida

CONTENTS

DARK WEBS

A Novella of Leda and Helen of Sparta

Part One

of

The Beautiful Woman has Come

Debra J Giuffrida

This is a work of fiction. Any referenced to real people, events, establishments, organizations or locales are intended only to give the fiction a sense of reality and authenticity. Other names, characters, and incidents are either a product of the author's imagination or are used fictitiously as are those fictionalized events and incidents which involve real persons and did not occur or are set in the future.

DARK WEBS

DEDICATION

To my mother.

CAST OF CHARACTERS

(In Order of Appearance)

Petepihu ~ Daughter of the king of Kemet and sister to **Amenhotep**
Amenhotep (Tepi) ~ Heir of the throne of Kemet
Mutemwiya ~ Mother of **Petepihu**
Aaped ~ Nurse to **Petepihu**
Thestios ~ Soldier who comes to take **Petepihu** to Sparta, husband to **Eurythemis** and **Petepihu**'s step-father
Eurythemis ~ Wife of **Thestios** and step mother of **Petepihu**
Leda ~ Queen of Laconia, wife of King **Tyndareus**, **Helen**'s mother. Formally **Petepihu** of Kemet
Diodorus ~ High Priest of Zeus in Laconia.
Tyndareus ~ King of Laconia, husband of **Leda**.
Thalis ~ Maid to Queen **Leda**
Menelaus ~ Husband of **Helen,** King of Laconia.
Aspasia ~ High Priestess of Hera in Laconia.
Nephele ~ High Priestess of Aphrodite in Laconia.
Polymnia ~ High Priestess of Athena in Laconia.
Alexandros-Paris ~ Prince of Ilion, son of King Priam of Ilion, youngest brother of **Hector** ~ Prince of Ilion.
Hector ~ Prince of Ilion, elder son of King Priam of Ilion, brother to Paris.
Helen ~ Queen of Laconia, wife of **Menelaus**, daughter of **Leda** an, some think, Zeus.
Arturos ~ Cousin of **Hector** and **Paris**, captain of the two princes' guards.
Clytemnestra ~ Sister of **Helen**, daughter of **Leda** and **Tyndareus**, wife of Agamemnon the brother of **Menelaus**.
Iphigeneia ~ Daughter of **Clytemnestra** and Agamemnon, **Helen**'s

niece.
Dorius ~ Acolyte of the god Hermes, appointed guardian of **Helen**.

AUTHOR'S NOTE

Without a doubt this is a work of fiction. And for those that are triggered by acts of sexual assault or sexual content of any kind may I caution you about this novella.

It is based on two Ancient Greek myths. The first is of Leda the beautiful queen of the king of Sparta who was assaulted by a god. The second is the tale of Helen, Leda's daughter and said to have been so beautiful that when she was abducted by the prince of Ilion (Troy) they launched a thousand ships to retrieve her. Poppycock.

In this telling there are no supernatural beings taking credit for wrecking the lives of the mortals that worship them. There are only real people with real feelings of love, lust, envy, anger, and sadness. I did try to follow the original tales, though a change of timelines was necessary to suit the story. As to the rest, I just used my fertile imagination.

A sudden blow: the great wings beating still
Above the staggering girl, her thighs caressed
But the dark webs, her nape caught in his bill,
He holds her helpless breast upon his breast.

~ William Butler Yeats, Leda and the Swan

MenNefer ~ Kemet

CHAPTER 1

For Maat

Her small bare feet slapped against the cold stone floor. The sound they made echoed down the length of the corridor. Giggles bubbled up her throat and tumbled out of her smile.

"Petepihu, don't make me chase you!" Exasperation pinched her nurse's voice.

An arm reached out from a side door and grabbed the girl, stopping her forward progress. Petepihu gasped.

"Hush."

She smiled; it was her older brother Amenhotep.

"Get in here." He closed the door behind her. The child wrenched her arm out of her brother's grasp and put her ear against the whitewashed surface, listening to the sound of her nurse complaining as she passed them by. The girl turned to face her brother.

"I think she's gone." Petepihu reached for the leather pull.

"No," he said softly, "don't go. Stay here with me. I brought food, look," the older boy pointed to a small table. There was a cone of fresh cheese, a round loaf of bread, a plate with purple grapes, and a blue enameled jar filled with something Petepihu could only hope was drinkable. "If they can't find you they can't send you away," her brother said.

"You know I don't want to go, Tepi, mother doesn't want me to go either, but," Petepihu knit her brow and sighed, "she won't defy father." Her mother had no real power, she was only a second wife, just raised up from a concubine due to the fact she was a king's son's mother. She walked over to the table, picked up the loaf of bread, and tore off a piece. She brought it to her nose, closed her eyes, and breathed in its nutty aroma. Amenhotep placed his hands on her shoulders. Her head reached just below his breast. He frowned, pursed his lips, and turned her around.

"Father shouldn't send any king's daughter to foreigners. It's against *Ma'at*." The prince's voice softened. "If I was sitting on the Throne of Geb I wouldn't send you, I'd marry you." His voice sounded thick, full of emotion. Petepihu loved her brother and knew he loved her but she was a king's daughter and had to obey her father. Tears sprang to her eyes. She sniffed and buried her face against her brother's chest.

"Marry me anyway, Tepi," she sobbed, wrapping her arms around her brother's muscular torso.

Amenhotep hugged his sister and kissed the top of her head. He wished it was that simple, but his sister had been promised to the King of Laconia, far off over the Great Green, and he did not have the power to go against the Lord of the Two Lands, their father.

"They have sent wondrous ships and wood and other gifts for you. Father can't go back on his word. *That* would be against *Ma'at*."

Petepihu leaned back, sniffed, and stared up at her brother. Her lashes were clumped together from her tears and the kohl that rimmed her large slanted eyes ran in streaks down her smooth cheeks.

"I know, mother said I must be a queen and live in a place called Sparta." The king's daughter stepped out of her brother's arms. "I am the youngest so it is my duty to go, for the good of Kemet. To preserve *Ma'at*." She looked at the door.

"I'll take you to Vizier Hepu," Tepi said with a sigh reaching over, running a thumb on her cheeks to wipe away the kohl.

Petepihu scrunched up her face.

"No, take me back to the *Khnr* and Aaped. I am sorry I ran from her." Petepihu scraped her upper lip with her teeth, glancing up at her brother from beneath her eyebrows.

A faint smile curled the king's son's lips.

"All right little monkey," Amenhotep's smile broadened.

~*~

Petepihu stood on the water steps under the sunshade next to her mother Mutemwiya, and Aaped, her nurse. Before them was a large foreign-looking boat secured to the docks with stout hemp ropes. The rowers were sitting with their oars shipped, and brightly colored banners, hanging from the rigging, snapped in the breeze.

The child reached up and stroked her new wig. When she woke she had been taken to the bathing room and her youth lock had been shorn. She had been given the wig and a grown women's headdress, it was a wide golden band circling her head, resting just above her eyebrows. Interspersed around the band were cornflowers made of gold with lapis lazuli centers, and encircling her neck hung a simple triple strand of gold wire with gold lotus blossoms hanging between lapis lazuli beads. The linen fabric of her new dyed blue *kalasiris* was woven with a fine gold-threaded zigzag pattern. Petepihu had never worn so much; it made her feel like she could truly be a queen, just like her mother. Her nurse fussed, adjusting the straps so they covered her thin child's chest.

"Let her alone, Aaped," Mutemwiya hissed at the nurse.

"Yes, Noble Lady." The woman pursed her lips and glared at the child but obeyed the king's wife.

A burly man disembarked from the ship; he was wearing a short-sleeved fringed linen tunic with a leather jerkin hanging down to mid-thigh, and around his waist was tied a leather apron. Slung across his muscular chest was a sword scabbard and he had a woolen cloak wrapped around his wide shoulders. In his meaty hand he carried a bronze helmet with red-feathered plumes. His hair hung in long, dark ringlets upon his shoulders; they glistened in the sun.

He approached the women and bent a knee.

"Rise, warrior." Mutemwiya took a step towards the man who obeyed her. He stood two heads above the king's wife.

"Greetings, Noble Lady Mutemwiya, I am Thestios of Pleuron." He turned to face the child. "And you must be the king's daughter, Petepihu." He smiled at the girl who blushed in return.

"My daughter is ready." The king's wife took hold of her child's hand and placed it within the hand of Thestios.

Sparta ~ Laconia

CHAPTER 2

A Sacrifice and a Wedding

Six Years Later ...

Petepihu stood straight and rigid as her maid adjusted the pleats of her wedding *peplos*, then draped a *himation* around the bride-to-be's shoulders, gathered and secured with a gold and pearl broach. With a quick bob of her head and a dip of her knee the maid retreated leaving Petepihu standing alone in her private rooms within the *gynaikonitis*.

Time had passed since she had arrived in Laconia, but she knew she would never forget where she had come from. Never forget the smell of the *Iteru* or the laughter of her sisters and brothers in the royal *Khnr*. Never forget her favorite cat or the pool choked with lotus in the center of her mother's garden. Never forget her brother, Tepi, now NebMa'atRa Amenhotep Heqawaset, Lord of the Two Lands, Mighty Bull, Great of Valor. A single tear welled up in each eye and threatened to ruin her carefully applied makeup. Petepihu sniffed and lightly dabbed each of them with a finger. On that finger was a ring. One perfect pearl graced the thick golden band. She stared at it, a wedding gift, from Tyndareus, her soon-to-be husband.

Eurythemis walked into the room, she was carrying a small bundle cradled in her hands. It was a short jewel-handled knife fashioned of electrum, she handed it Petepihu. The girl unwrapped the bundle and stared at the weapon within then glanced up at the woman who had taken the role of her mother since her arrival.

"You will perform the ritual sacrifice, the *proteleia*, to the goddess Aphrodite when the sun it high in the sky. Thestios has secured a pure white bull calf and I am sure the goddess will bless this marriage." Eurythemis fussed with the girl's *himation*. The woolen cloak was dyed a brilliant blue, it's edges embroidered with saffron colored flowers. "An Aegyptos ship arrived."

Petepihu's eyes widen and her heartbeat quickened. She was afraid to hope, that perhaps her brother would send *medjay* to bring her home.

"Your brother has sent gifts," Thestios said. "They are very beautiful. The dagger you hold is from him."

The girl looked again at the blade, she sniffed back the tears that again threatened to spill from her eyes.

"He also sent a pure white mare." The elder woman paused, waiting for some happy reaction from the girl who stood so still, only sadness registering on her lovely face. "Her groom says she is trained to a chariot."

Petepihu looked up at her Laconian mother. "I love horses, he remembered." The girl's lower lip trembled. The queen placed a hand on her adopted daughter's shoulder.

"Tyndareus is a good man. You will be happy as I am happy with your father, do not be so sad, daughter."

Petepihu looked at Eurythemis and sighed.

"I know mother, I will grow to love him, just as you love father. Tyndareus has been kind to me, now it is my turn to be kind to him. It is for *Ma'at* that I am here, I will not disgrace my real father, true of voice, and my real mother." The girl inhaled deeply then hugged Eurythemis. "I have grown to love you too and will miss you and father."

~*~

On the steps of Aphrodite's temple Thestios, Eurythemis and Petepihu stood. Tyndareus approached leading the pure white bull calf by a silver halter rope. Draped around the calf's neck was a garland of roses intertwined with small white bell-shaped flowers. Following behind the king was Aphrodite's Priestess Thera, the goddess' seer Efimia, the elderly Priest of Zeus

Hypatios, his young acolyte Diodorus, the Priestess of Hera, and the Priestess of Athena.

The high born of Lacedaemon, the ladies jewels and the men's weapons sparkling in the sunlight, drew up in a tight semi-circle; each vying for the best view of the Laconian king's new bride.

The calf bawled for its mother and tugged on the silver rope. Tyndareus jerked back and motioned for his bride-to-be to approach. Petepihu descended the temple's steps and walked up to him. This would be the first sacrifice they would perform together.

Tyndareus handed the rope to Thera and the priestess snugged the calf close, Hypatios stepped up on the far side of the animal, ready to come to her aid, should she need it.

With trembling fingers Petepihu raised the electrum blade. Tyndareus wrapped his hand around hers; he smiled. She returned the smile and lowered her eyes, looking at his large hand so rough and brown compared to hers; small, smooth skinned.

"My Lady, it is time," Priestess Thera said, smiled at Petepihu, and nodded her head.

Petepihu looked at the calf's large shining brown eyes. Deep within she thought she saw herself, tied between two forces, unable to move, awaiting what fate had to deliver. Tyndareus pulled on her hand but she held fast. She couldn't bring herself to cut the calf's throat.

"No," she whimpered, gritting her teeth, tears sprang to her eyes. "I can't."

"You must," Tyndareus snarled, his voice low and threatening. Petepihu looked up into his eyes, they were as black and deep as the calf's eyes. "You must," he repeated.

Petepihu looked at the calf, the priestess, and the priest then back at Tyndareus. Each person held the look of expectancy, waiting for her to make the first cut.

"Just nick his throat, I'll do the rest." His eyes had softened and a slight smile curled the ends of his lips. The girl looked back at the calf and allowed the king to move her hand to the animal's throat. She felt the resistance of the calf's hide and where the knife cut a thin oozing red line appeared.

The acolyte, Diodorus, appeared with a shallow silver bowl and placed it under the calf's throat. Tyndareus took the blade from Petepihu's hand and slashed the animal's throat open and its blood gushed into the waiting vessel.

~*~

Laughter reverberated within the *megaron*, the quad-pillared public audience chamber, at its center the great fire burned within the pit, the scented smoke curling towards the open ceiling past the second story gallery. As many times as there were voices to utter them, the wedding guests raised their cups to toast the bride and groom.

Petepihu sat next to her new husband Tyndareus and fidgeted with her wine cup. She twirled it and honeyed wine sloshed onto the table, staining the marble top. Tyndareus reached over and stilled her hand with a gentle squeeze. Petepihu tried to extract her hand but her husband held fast. A frown creased her forehead and she bit her bottom lip and pulled again, but Tyndareus squeezed her hand harder, she squeaked in pain and Eurythemis glared at the king.

"What are you doing?" the queen hissed, leaning over her adopted daughter and extracting the girl's hand from her husband's fist. "They are watching you." Eurythemis looked at Tyndareus with ice-cold eyes. The king smiled with pursed lips, raised an eyebrow, and wiped his hand on his thigh.

"It is time," Tyndareus said, pushed back his chair, and stood up. "My new bride is tired, I believe it is time for us to retire," his voice was loud so as to be heard over the sound of knowing laughter and cheers.

~*~

The door to the king's chambers swung shut on its leather hinges. Oil braziers had been lit and they cast their circles of light about the room. The scent of warm olive oil, mixed with the aroma of crushed lavender, chamomile, as well as frankincense from across the Great Waters, permeated the room.

Tyndareus sat on an armed chair in a dim corner watching as two servants removed his bride's clothing. First they unclasped the *himation*, and then untied the belt from around her *peplos*. Petepihu raised her arms and the women slipped the straps of the tiered gown from off her shoulders; it puddled to the ground around her leather sandal shod feet.

While one servant removed her sandals, the other untwined her hair and arranged it about her bare shoulders. Finished, the two bowed, first to their king and then to their new queen and slipped out of the room.

Tyndareus rose and walked up to his wife and took a lock of her hair between his fingers, brought it to his nose, and sniffed.

"You smell delicious." He stood before her naked and his desire for her was evident. Petepihu's mother had told her what to expect, so she was not surprised when her husband cupped her breasts and rolled her nipples between his thumbs and forefingers.

"Lovely, just lovely."

He tilted her head up and kissed her, thrusting his tongue between her lips. Breaking off the kiss, Tyndareus scooped her up and carried her to the bed. Placing her in the center, he positioned himself between her legs. For several moments he just stared at her, his eyes feasting on her naked flesh, then he ran his hands up the insides of her thighs and cupped her sex. The girl closed her eyes and tried to swallow her anxiety away. The wine she had consumed at the feast should have relaxed her, but it hadn't.

"I will be slow and easy with you, my lovely, I want you to want me as much as I desire you."

Tyndareus was true to his word. He used his mouth and fingers to arouse her. And when she was slick with desire he entered her.

~*~

The morning sun knifed long golden arms into the king's chamber. As it rose, those warm arms caressed the young queen as she slumbered.

A servant set a tray of figs, cheese, and fresh baked bread on a table near the window, momentarily blocking the sun, casting a shadow. Petepihu roused, knuckled her eyes, blinked, and opened them wide.

"The king sends his regards and wishes you to remain abed as long as you desire, my queen." The maid smiled and nodded her head.

Petepihu felt her cheeks warm and knew she was blushing. Her husband had teased moans from deep within her body as her pleasure heightened. His own roar at the moment he spilled his seed had reverberated around the high-ceilinged chamber.

As the maid's smile broadened, the queen knew that everyone had heard.

CHAPTER 3

Leda

"I refuse to have a queen with an Aegyptos name. Hence forth your name will be Leda." Tyndareus slipped his arms through his leather jerkin and secured it. He turned and faced his wife sitting upon a chair in her private rooms in the gynaikonitis, her hands resting on the swell of her belly. "Did you hear me?"

Petepihu, looked up at her husband. "Yes, my name is now Leda. Is that all? I wish to bathe," the queen said her words terse. The transformation was now complete. She could speak, read, and write Mycenaean, and now, given a Laconian name, she must cast off all remnants of her former life. The child growing in her belly would never know their Kemeteyu heritage, never know the beauty of the *Iteru* as it flowed down the length of her home land, never know of the greatness of her forebears nor the monuments they built to their eternal godhood. A deep sadness filled her heart. She did not feel love for Tyndareus, only a sense of duty. The child within her womb stirred.

Her husband and king walked up to where she sat and rested a hand on top of both of hers.

"This child is of my blood. No Aegyptos words will he speak, no Aegyptos gods will he worship. He will be suckled at the breast of a Spartan, not yours." He gripped her hands and she looked up at him, her teeth clenched against the pain as he squeezed. "By Zeus you will obey me." His eyes were hard and black beneath his thick brows.

"Yes," the word came out in a hiss. Tyndareus relaxed his grip and smiled, raising her fingers to his lips. "Then all will be well. I believe you should make sacrifice to Hera for a healthy boy, without delay." He let go the young queen's hands and cupped the mound of the growing child within her. "Yes, with her blessing you will birth a fine, strong son." His voice had grown wistful.

Tyndareus straightened up, pulled on the hem of his jerkin, and squared his shoulders.

Leda rubbed her hands easing the pain from her husband's rough handling. She couldn't help wondering why he had agreed to accept a bride from Aegyptos, as he called her homeland, her Kemet, the Black Lands, named such for the rich fertile black earth that the *Iteru* deposited upon its banks during the season of *Akhet* when the goddess Aset's tears caused the river to overflow. Closing her eyes, she could almost smell the loamy moist mineral-rich soil.

She felt tears threaten, her throat thickened and her heart ached for her lost home, her family, and most of all her brother Tepi. Tyndareus must have sensed her sorrow for he raised her chin with rough fingers.

"Look at me."

She obeyed him.

"Leda, you are my wife and the queen of Laconia. You are carrying my son. You should be standing at my side proud and strong not whimpering here in your chambers."

"Yes, my lord." Leda tried to pull her face out of his hand but he held fast.

"Grow up, little girl. You are safe within my care; no harm will come to you. Stop pining for what can never be. Accept your fate and learn to be a good obedient wife." He let go her face. "Now get up and perform your duties, sacrifice to the gods, oversee the running of my house, and learn to weave for Zeus' sake." He stopped, pursed his lips, and shook his head. "What do you women do in Aegyptos? Eat lotus blossoms and drink wine all day? I will not have a useless lazy woman."

Tyndareus turned and strode to the door, wrested it open and stepped into the hall.

"Where is that girl of yours? Thalis, isn't that her name?" He asked looking into Leda's bedchamber then back down the hall. “Thalis! Attend your mistress!” His voice boomed and echoed down the plaster-walled corridor. The sound of bare feet slapping on the cold floor grew louder and louder until Thalis stood in front of the king.

She dropped to her knees and bowed her head.

“Get up, you useless chit.” Tyndareus hissed at the young servant.

“As you command, my king.”

Leda saw the king’s eyes linger on her maid’s breasts and she felt her stomach flutter with jealousy. She did not love him but he was hers. She continued to watch as Thalis looked up at the king from beneath her thick black lashes, a sly smile curling her full lips.

“Come with me husband,” Leda stretched out her arm, wagging her hand at her husband. “Come with me to make sacrifice to the gods. Hold my hand as you did when we were wed.” Leda was watching her husband, searching his face for any show of his continued desire of her. The fact that she looked for that desire shocked her. Before this she would have wished for his quick departure, leaving her to spend the day alone and undisturbed. A wave of irritation washed over her and she stood, reaching out her hand, beckoning her king to attend her, his queen.

“Perhaps the gods will be more favorable if we do it as one.” Leda forced a wane smile. “Then you can share the mid-day meal with me, yes?”

Tyndareus looked away from the blushing servant and over at his wife; he nodded.

“Fair enough.”

~*~

Within the empty temple a brisk wind whipped around soaring marble columns stirring loose leaves into a whirl, the dry sound of their movement echoed within the cold hall, accentuating the vastness.

The aroma of old burnt incense and rancid oil assailed the royal couple as they stepped into Zeus' home in Sparta. The sound of their sandal-shod footsteps drew the priest and his accolade from within the temple's recesses.

Hypatios shuffled towards Tyndareus and the newly named Leda. Following behind the old bent-back priest was his young accolade, Diodorus.

"Greetings your majesties," the priest spoke spreading his arms wide in welcome. The accolade stopped behind his mentor and bowed his head, looking up under his dark brows at Queen Leda, a hint of a smile curling his lips.

"Greetings Hypatios, how fare the gods pleasure?" Tyndareus put his hands on his hips. He hadn't noticed Diodorus ogling his wife, but Leda had noticed. She licked her lips and quickly looked away. She felt her cheeks burn.

Tyndareus took hold her hand and drew it to his chest.

"We are here to dedicate our unborn son to Zeus."

"But that is a momentous occasion, we should have time to prepare, I cannot possibly procure a white he goat for the sacrifice!" The priest wrung his hands, his voice rising as did his creased brow. Tyndareus pressed his lips into a hard flat line.

"I see."

Leda squeaked as Tyndareus inadvertently squeezed her hand tighter than he had intended. The king glanced down at his wife and with a huff he let loose her hand.

"How long do you need to prepare?" Tyndareus glared at the priest who wrung his hands, licked his lips, and bobbed his head.

"Give me two rises of the sun, your majesty. It will give me plenty of time to get the goat and—."

"Fine, you have two days, make it happen." Tyndareus grabbed for Leda's hand and the two left the priest and his accolade standing in front of the temple.

~*~

Two days later, as good as his word, Hypatios arranged for

his king and queen to sacrifice to Zeus.

A brisk chilled wind whipped the priests' robes around their bodies as they stood squinting in the harsh winter sunlight. The old priest stood next to his accolade Diodorus who held the halter rope of the white he goat. Leda and Tyndareus approached the priests. The queen was snuggly wrapped in a long lynx-fur cape.

A blast of wind sent a loose branch with dry brittle leaves skittering along the open portico where the party stood. It caused the goat to rear on its hind legs and struggle to free himself from Diodorus' hold. The goat bleated and dropped its head pulling back. With a great heave it pushed Diodorus sending the accolade tumbling onto the ground. The halter rope slipped through his fingers and the he goat was free.

Zeus' priest gasped, his mouth and eyes wide with horror. The old man reached out to his accolade. Tyndareus turned and roared in anger, Leda squealed, grabbing her belly, as her husband pushed her aside. Diodorus jumped to his feet and took off at a run after the errant he goat.

"My Lord," Hypatios said in a ragged whisper. He dropped to his knees, his face pale, clutching his left arm.

~*~

Diodorus stopped running when he was out of sight of the temple. *Stupid goat*, he thought, would the old priest beat him for choosing such an animal. He was far too old to accept a chiding such as young boys receive. He kicked a rock and huffed. He spied the blasted goat cropping tufts of grass at the end of the lane, the halter rope still attached and wrapped around its hind legs.

~*~

Diodorus dragged the stubborn animal back to the temple. When he stepped into the portico he came up short. The king and queen were gone but priests and priestesses from the other gods were standing over the supine body of Hypatios.

The first to see him was the priestess of Hera. She had been kneeling at the old priests side.

"Ah, Diodorus, come, help us move your master."

The accolade stood still not understanding what was happening.

"Hypatios is dead, Diodorus. Come, help us," the priest of Hades said. A look of shock spread over the accolade's face. "Give the goat to Thera and come here. We need your strength."

Diodorus did as he was told and knelt beside his deceased master. Seeing his mentor lying here, this man who had been the closest thing to a father, seeing him in death was almost too much for him to bare. He sniffed and as he helped the priest of Hades lift Hypatios he felt a tear slip down his cheek.

~*~

Without a confirmed priest of Zeus to preside over sacrifices and feast days the royal household was in a state of fear. Zeus was known to be a jealous god, one who sent thunderbolts down from the heavens for even the smallest of slights. Here his priest had died while in the performance of a sacrifice to curry his favor, what the king of the gods would do was speculated on by all the serving staff and the minor lords and ladies.

Leda was one of the only royals that did not worry about Zeus and what he would or could do to them. He wasn't her god. Her child grew in her belly and that was all she cared about. Whether it was a boy to please Tyndareus was all she felt was important. Not what some imaginary god would or wouldn't do because some silly goat had ran off causing this god's priest to die. The goat had been sacrificed as planned so she couldn't see what the problem was. All she felt had to be done was appoint another priest. That was Tyndareus' problem, not hers. And it was a small problem. Her father had done it all the time. She was sure that her husband had relatives that needed an important post. Why didn't he just set one of them up as Zeus' priest. She posed that very question to Tyndareus that evening.

"It is not that easy, wife. We need to have a seer read the

portents and make sacrifices on the right days. More than one may be called for." He said pacing back and forth.

"The old priest had an accolade, did he not? Why not just appoint him?"

Tyndareus stopped mid stride and looked at his wife over his shoulder.

"At least until a seer can throw her bones or read the entrails of some poor animal," Leda said. "You are the king. Why not make it so?" Without answering her Tyndareus walked away leaving her sitting among her ladies maids.

~*~

A vase sailed through the air and crashed against the wall of Leda's bed chamber.

"This is what I get for listening to a woman! And a foreign woman at that!" Tyndareus growled at the assembled midwives and his wife who lay on her bed holding her daughter.

"This is what I get for a bungled sacrifice. A dead priest and a girl child! You were supposed to birth me sons woman!" He strode over to her bed pushing a young midwife out of the way and grabbed for the child cradled in Leda's arms.

"No!" Leda screamed enfolding her daughter closer, trying to keep Tyndareus from taking her away.

"Give that to me! I'll sacrifice it to Zeus, then maybe he will give me the son I desire!"

"You touch one hair on her head and I swear I will call down the wrath of my gods! The gods of Kemet, every last one of them! They will give me the strength to make a sacrifice of you!" Leda spit out the angry words from between clenched teeth. Tyndareus paused, his hands still reaching for the child. "She is your daughter as much as mine. How could you threaten to kill her? Besides," Leda paused and licked her lips, "your goddess Hera gave her to you. Thera, her priestess told me this very day of her birth. Are you willing to anger one goddess to placate one god? Hera has named her too, she is Clytemnestra." Tyndareus put his hands down and stood upright. His face was still contorted with rage but Leda saw that it was starting to ease.

"The priestess told you this?" he asked.

"Yes, you can question her if you wish or you can believe me, your wife, this child's mother."

Tyndareus ran his hand over his face and turned his back to his wife and daughter.

"Very well. But you had better give me a son." Without looking at them the king left his queen's chamber, slamming the door behind him.

CHAPTER 4

Leda and the Swan

The palace was aglow with riotous light. Inside, torches blazed from sconces circling the vast high-ceilinged banquet hall. The wealthy and well positioned of Lacedaemon stood, sat, or reclined within. Queen Leda lay upon her gilded couch and the loud sonance of feasting rolled over her slender body, cloaking her. Over all this she felt hungry eyes turned toward her. She knew whose they were.

With a lift of her chin, she casually scanned the room, at last resting her eyes on Diodorus, the priest of Zeus. He stood apart from the revelers and his dark-lashed eyes stared back at her. She watched the muscles in his square jaw clench and the nostrils of his aquiline nose flare, as if he had caught a faint whiff of her perfume. His brazenness sent a shiver the length of her body. A bubble of desire fluttered in her stomach as she watched the tip of his tongue slip from between his firm lips, lick them, and disappear. His white priest's cloak fluttered and caught her eye as he wrapped it about his muscular shoulders. It draped, running liquid over his slender hips and muscular thighs. He slid a hand down the cloak's length, revealing his desire. Her heartbeat quickened and she felt a flush of heat rise to warm her cheeks.

Thalis, her maid, tapped her on the hand and into it the maid pressed a golden cup. Leda brought the cup to her lips, not removing her eyes from the priest.

"Diodorus sends the God's wine to you, with his compliments," Thalis said and sat on the floor, snatching a morsel of food from her mistress' plate.

Leda ignored her maid's impertinence and allowed one sip

of the ruby liquid to flow over her lips and tongue. The wine was sweetened with honey, yet she tasted something else, a flavor she could not identify. It was bitter, not to her liking. She sipped again; the foreignness of the flavor was more pronounced. With a frown she set the cup down and wiped her mouth with the back of her hand.

She turned her attention to her husband, Tyndareus, seated next to her, as a young noblewoman pressed her ample breasts against his arm; the woman whispered in his ear. He threw back his head and roared with laughter, turned to Leda, reached over, squeezed her thigh, and patted it. She smiled at her husband and looked back into the crowd. The priest had vanished.

She picked up the cup of the God's wine and handed it back to her maid. The maid drank of it; Leda frowned.

With a grin Thalis raised a slender eyebrow, "It will bring ill luck if we waste libations gifted from the Gods," she said as she set the now empty cup on a passing servant's tray.

"Truly." Leda raised a hand to her lips, and it came away wet with perspiration. "Attend me, I need a cool breeze, the God's wine has gone straight to my head." Leda allowed Thalis to help her rise from the couch. The odor of spilt Aegyptos beer and Mycenaean wine mixed with the fug of sweating bodies made Leda's stomach lurch and the room whirl before her eyes. Fresh air, she was sure, was all she needed.

~*~

Laughter and boisterous feasting spilled forth from archways and windows onto the surrounding gardens. The Queen ambled down toward a small lake that stretched out in front of Aphrodite's temple. Six pure-white swans glided over the calm surface of the water, and their contrails sparkled under the light of the moon hanging full and lush surrounded by twinkling stars.

Leda sat down hard on the soft grass at the water's edge and layback, throwing an arm over her eyes.

"Is all well, my Queen?" It was Diodorus; he stood over her, his face in deep shadow.

Leda made to sit up but stopped and groaned. "Yes," she mouthed the lie.

"You appear in distress. Allow me." He lifted her, cradled her, and walked her over to a small outcropping of stone and set her down in a copse of soft grass. "I have waited for a moment such as this," he whispered. His breath was hot and moist against her throat.

"You take liberties," she said around a tongue that felt twice its normal size. Diodorus knelt in front of her; his face swam before her eyes. She swiped at them hoping to clear her vision. "Where am I?"

"You are safe with me, my beloved." The priest rose, he took Leda's chin in his hand and tipped it up. His lips were hot as they pressed against hers. He thrust his tongue between her lips; he tasted of cinnamon and wine. His hands dropped to her shoulders, and he pushed her sheer *chitin* down, exposing her firm breasts. He cupped each and caressed her soft skin. She titled her head and arched her back as he took a firm nipple between his teeth and flicked it with his tongue. Her breath caught in her throat, she tried to move away, but found she could not, nor did she wish to.

Ripples of desire puckered her skin. She had wondered long what his mouth would feel like upon her. She had dreamt of it and now it was happening. Her heart raced with fear, yet the thrill of the forbidden caused her stomach to clench, and she felt herself become slick with need. He let go her breast and sat back pushing her clothing from her body, laying her naked before him. Diodorus' face wavered in and out of her vision and his features seemed to change. Before her wine-fogged eyes, she thought he became the very deity he served. He stood erect before her, handsome as a god. Here was Zeus himself making claim to her body. The priest spread her legs and fell upon her.

"Love me mighty Zeus," Leda whispered. Diodorus grinned.

~*~

Thalis had staggered down toward the lake only to fall against an ash tree. As she clasped it firmly, she squeezed her eyes closed wishing the world to stop spinning. Moments passed and she heard voices, but something was not right, they sounded queer to her ear. Cautiously she opened one eye and peered around the tree trunk.

Standing over her Queen she saw a huge man. An aura of brilliant white light surrounded him. The trumpet of a male swan sliced through the still night air. The man had her Queen in his arms, but they didn't look like arms, they looked like giant wings. She shook her head, and everything started to whirl. The ground heaved and once again she squeezed her eyes shut, grasping the tree. She heard the flap of mighty wings and the splash of water and again a male swan trumpeted. Slowly she opened first one eye then the other and watched in horror, as this man seemed to turn himself into a giant swan; he must be a god. The maid swiped at her eyes, and there in front of her under the glowing moon what she imagined was an otherworldly swan took Queen Leda.

~*~

Tyndareus rested his elbow on his knee and leaned forward. He watched a guard drag the young woman by her upper arm toward him as he sat upon his throne in the receiving hall. Her thin *chitin* slipped up her thighs revealing soft flesh. Had he bed this one? He couldn't remember. As they neared, he frowned and snorted through his nose. This was his wife's maid. She was voicing her disapproval for the ill treatment his guard was giving her. Her shrill ululations reverberated off the high ceiling making him wince. He stood.

"Silence!"

The single word filled the hall and the maid's head swung around. She cowered, hanging from the guard's hand. He yanked her to her feet and marched down the remainder of the hall, finally stopping in front of the dais. He let her go and she fell to her knees, her head upon the cold marble floor.

Tyndareus sat upon his golden throne, his back straight, chin jutting out.

"Get up." His staccato words were flat and contained none of the emotions that swirled through his body.

Thalis obeyed her master.

"I have done nothing wrong, your majesty! Please, have mercy," the maid sobbed clasping her hands together imploring her innocence to the king.

"Repeat for me this tale you are spreading about my queen." Tyndareus narrowed his eyes, glared at the maid, and clenched his jaw, trying hard to contain the hot anger he felt well up inside him.

Thalis glanced about and wet her lips.

"It's the truth, I tell you, I saw him, I saw Zeus himself." Thalis stopped, swallowed, and wrung her hands. "One moment he was the priest Diodorus, the next he was our god Zeus and he turned himself into a swan! Truly I saw this."

"Did you say you saw the priest of Zeus before you saw the god?"

Thalis nodded her head several times, tears running unchecked down her cheeks. "The god appeared and spread his arms and became a magnificent swan. I heard him trumpet before he took our sweet queen." The maid buried her face in her hands, her shoulders shaking as she wept.

With a wave of his hand Tyndareus commanded the guard to remove the maid.

"She is free to go back to the queen. Return with the priest."

"As you command," the guard said with a dip of his head and a fist crossed over his leather-clad breast.

~*~

Tyndareus watched the guard and maid leave. He knew there had been no god, no swan, only Diodorus. But had his wife been compliant in their coupling? Only the priest and his wife knew, and he refused to question her.

The room was empty as he wished no one about while he

dealt with this problem. More ears attached to wagging tongues he did not need. And so, he heard the heavy echoing steps of the man who had seduced his queen. Every fiber of his body quivered with rage as did the urge to jump down and sever the priest's head from his body.

Tyndareus clenched the arms of his golden throne, his knuckles white. The late afternoon sun streamed into the vast room bathing the king in celestial light.

Diodorus stood below the dais his head held high and his shoulders squared. His priestly robes glowed white and Tyndareus could see how the maid, drunk on wine, could mistake him for the god he served.

Tyndareus sat back and scrutinized him. Perhaps there was some truth to the maid's story, perhaps not. But a swan? He planned on giving the priest the opportunity to clarify that point.

"Do you understand why I have you here before me?"

The priest raised his chin, his lips pressed into a straight line, staring at a point just above the king's head. The silence in the chamber further angered Tyndareus. He stood up and unsheathed the great sword from the scabbard that lay against the throne. The rasp as the blade exiting the leather sheath echoed dully within the vast chamber. A shaft of sunlight glinted off the polished honed blade as he raised the tip to touch just under the priest's chin.

"You played the god with my queen and took what was not yours. Even common thieves know the price of theft," he paused to see if his words had any effect upon the priest. Tyndareus' nostrils flared, anger rose within his breast filling his chest and consuming all the breath within, yet the man before him remained silent. "Payment is due, priest."

Tyndareus grasped the hilt with two hands and swung. Diodorus' head fell to the clean swept floor with a hollow plop. The priest's dead eyes didn't see his body crumple to the floor at Tyndareus' feet.

~*~

The inner chamber of the *gynaikonitis* glowed from a single shaft of sunlight streaming through the large window that faced the courtyard. Leda could hear water running into the pool that was the centerpiece of the woman's private palace. She could also hear heavy footsteps drawing near her rooms. With a quick intake of breath, she rose from her bed and dashed to the door, swinging it wide.

Tyndareus approached adjusting his jerkin. His attention was on his clothing and not his trajectory. Leda frowned, clenched her jaw, and wondered which of her ladies' chamber he had just exited. She eased a smile onto her lips as she stepped out into the courtyard.

As he drew abreast of her, she reached out and took his arm. He stopped and glanced down at her fingers.

"You have not been to my bed since the night of the banquet, my husband." She tried to make her voice sound gay and lighthearted.

Standing next to his thick muscular body she felt small and helpless but would not let her fear show. He raised his eyes. Leda saw the thing she most dreaded deep within their dark brown depths. Disgust, yes, it was there and in the set of his jaw too. Her hand flew to her stomach, fingers protectively splayed over the growing swell of the child she hoped he had put there.

"And you shall not see me." Tyndareus removed her hand from his arm and bowed his head before turning his back on her.

A chill ran the length of her body and she stepped back into her empty rooms leaning against the now closed door. The growing darkness as the sun slipped behind the hills filled her with dread. Memories flooded her, memories of when she first came here to Sparta to be Tydareus' queen. She had felt this same fear. Fear of being alone.

~*~

Night after night Leda would stand at her door, her cheek resting against the cool wood, eyes closed waiting to hear

Tyndareus' footsteps. Standing in the dark, it wasn't until moon rise that she would hear him near her chamber. At first her heart fluttered with hope, but as each night he continued to pass, never even pausing, her expectations diminished until she stopped waiting for him.

The months passed, the child grew heavy within her, but her feelings of dread did not. Two nights after Tyndareus departed to quell a land dispute on the far side of the Valley pains of imminent childbirth clenched Leda's belly.

~*~

Outside the birthing chamber several wives of prominent politicians and military men stood waiting to see the results of the royal birth. None had been invited in to bear witness.

"Zeus? Perhaps, perhaps not. She says it wasn't but that maid of hers said she saw the god with her very own eyes."

"But why a swan?"

"They are beloved of his daughter Aphrodite, and she *is* the goddess of love."

"Yes, but...."

"We will see, won't we? If the babe looks like Tyndareus we will have our answer."

"If it's a girl, let's hope the father *is* Zeus!"

~*~

Inside the midwives prepared for the birth. Leda was being walked about the room by two of their number. Each time a contraction started the young Queen doubled over, gritting her teeth, grasping the midwives' hands, clenching them, her knuckles white.

"You must walk more, my Lady. It will ease the pain and make the babe come sooner." Leda's water had not yet broken, and the midwives worried that something was amiss with the birth. They were afraid the child was not right or worse.

It was Leda's second child, as she had a girl, Clytemnestra, by Tyndareus just three years prior. It had been a difficult birth and fear of this being the same was written on her face. The contraction subsided and Leda smiled weakly and proceeded to walk.

Much to the midwives relief the child wasn't long in coming. After an hour of pacing the pains were stronger and but moments apart. The midwives led Leda to the birthing chair. The eldest of them crouched in front and reached up with a sharp knife to make a cut so that the queen's skin would not tear, but the child was small, and its head crested and slid into the waiting woman's hands.

With a gasp the midwife stood up, holding the baby in front of her, at arm's length still attached to Leda's womb.

"The child, it's in an egg!" She presented the babe to the other woman. Whispers of "Zeus" reached the queen's ears. The tiny newborn was enveloped in a translucent shimmering membrane, as if Leda had truly birthed a young swan's first egg.

"Give me my baby!" Leda said as she lurched forward.

"Break it open!" A younger midwife reached for the baby but the elder moved the *en caul* child out of her reach.

"Let the mother do it!" another of the midwives hissed. The elder saw the wisdom and handed the cloaked baby to Leda. With trembling fingers, the Queen ripped at the membrane and uncovered her daughter.

CHAPTER 5

Helen ~ Desire and Deceit

Sixteen summers later...

The man who was her king and husband walked out of her bedchamber without a backward glance. Her tear-filled eyes followed his retreating back. He always left her when the sun was rising, when its red-gold light knifed its way into her room, brightening the dim interior, pushing away the dark of the night.

Helen shivered under her blanket and pulled it up to her chin. She wanted to burrow into her bed and forget. Forget his hands, his grunts and groans, and his seed wet between her thighs. She wanted to forget that her womb was empty, and he would return each night until he filled it.

She listened as birds chirped outside her window and watched as a fly lit on an edge of a table, preening its long proboscis with its front legs. She wondered how everything could seem so calm, so beautiful when she felt so ugly, so dirty.

Little Myrine slipped into Helen's room carrying a tray of olives, fresh baked bread, goat's milk cheese, and a carafe. The girl smiled at her queen and set the tray on a table shooing the fly with a linen cloth, a frown creasing her forehead.

"Do you wish me to stay, my lady?" the girl asked. The young queen shook her head and swiped at her eyes.

"No, I'll join you in the bathing room, our foot race is first."

"Yes, my lady, I remember, my sisters have spoken of nothing else since the temple was finished," the girl smiled and hugged herself searching the face of her queen. Myrine frowned "Do you want me to send for Thalis?" She had noticed her queen's tears and the dark circles under her glistening eyes. Helen shook her head again and mouthed a silent 'no.'

Helen threw back the woven blanket and rose from her bed walking toward the tray of food and the lithe young girl. She rolled the olives around with a slender finger; picking up the small loaf of warm bread, tore off a hunk and brought it to her nose, closed her eyes, and inhaled. The tangy scent filled her head erasing the fug of sex and the disgust at the reek of another's perfume on her husband's sweat covered body.

Myrine took up the carafe and poured her mistress a cup, handing it to her. Helen opened her eyes, smiled, and accepted the beverage, brought it to her lips then frowned.

She wrinkled her nose, "What is this?"

"Red clover and nettles and wild mint with a dollop of honey, Mother says it will make you, make your, make uh," the girl stumbled over her words, a blush rising to her cheeks. "It will help you have a child," she finished with a deep breath, her eyes looking right then left, shuffling her feet in embarrassment.

Helen smiled at Myrine's discomfort. "You may go now, Myrine, I'm quite fine." She had noticed earlier the look of worry in the girl's eyes. "You seem to be the only one who cares," she said into her cup of tea, almost too soft for the girl to hear.

"I love you, my lady." Myrine reached out her hand, a weak smile curling her lips. With a sigh the girl let her arm drop to her side.

"I know you do." Helen smiled in an attempt to erase the mood of gloom. "Shoo, be off with you, make sure that my *peplos* is clean and without blemish. I don't want to offend the goddess."

"May Olympus forbid it" Myrine said with a sharp intake of breath. She smiled and bowed before leaving her queen standing by the open window, bathed in the light of the morning sun.

The sounds of morning floated through the window on a fresh breeze. Helen's senses seemed heightened. Setting the cup of tea on the table she turned her back on the room and looked out the window at the new temple sitting high above the palace. It glowed in the morning sun as if it were constructed of solid gold, not pure white marble. When the sun was at mid sky, she would be standing next to her husband raising the knife to make sacrifice to the temple's goddess—Hera, who had cursed her, kept her womb empty all out of jealousy. Or so said the seers and the priestess' and her mother. Helen had been raised to believe in the gods, the goddesses. She had heard the whispers, seen the sidelong glances of the women at court. Was she truly Zeus' daughter? Her mother had neither denied nor confirmed the rumors. She had died never revealing the truth.

And her father Tyndareus, he had also been silent on the truth of her parentage. Did he believe that her mother had birthed a god's child? He had loved her; she was sure of it. Did he believe that she was his own true daughter?

Helen turned back to the room. She did not feel special, God-like. Walking toward the table, which held her pots of cosmetics, she raised a polished copper disc and gazed at her reflection. Turning her head slightly, back and forth, she tried to see if the young woman before her held any indication of being a child of mighty Zeus. Her fingers strayed to her cheek, and she watched as they traced the outline of her lips.

They called her Helen the beautiful, Helen the lovely, she of the perfect complexion, so many compliments. Perhaps a god truly sired her, to make everyone who gazed upon her either desire her or envy her. And the reason her father could give her to a man like Menelaus.

"If you stare at yourself long enough the gods will turn you into a flower!"

Helen dropped the mirror with a gasp.

Thalis, her mother's old servant stood with her hands on her ample hips, a frown adding creases to her age-wrinkled face.

If she were a flower at least when she was crushed underfoot, she wouldn't feel the pain.

~*~

High on a promontory, a temple's brilliant white columns

stood gleaming against an intense blue Laconian sky. A light breeze blew a dry leaf skittering along the clean floor as the early morning sun cast long fingered shadows into the elegant building. Long after the final craftsman had left, the smell of rock dust still hung suspended in the air, mixing with the aroma of fresh-turned earth from the newly planted roses that dotted the entrance of the vast new edifice, built for Hera, queen of the gods of Mount Olympus. Dewdrops sparkled on those perfect blood-red roses and their perfume wafted in the wake of King Menelaus as he marched into the temple.

Aspasia, Hera's priestess, her back against a painted marble statue of the goddess, watched her king. His strides slowed and took on an even cadence. With a curt nod he swept past her and stopped, hands on his hips, surveying the vast inner hall with its intricate mosaic commanding the entire floor. The vivid pieces of fired clay produced a portrait of the goddess and what one could only imagine Mount Olympus might be. His mouth curled with pleasure and his eyes gleamed with pride as he bent his head to look at the masterpiece. The design had been his vision. The priestess' eyes followed her king as he moved off walking from shadow to sunlight, his deep red hair gleaming as the sun's rays caught the curls tight against his head, a single golden circlet resting upon his brow.

"All must be ready for the dedication ceremony, Aspasia. The queen will be joining me, and all eyes will be upon us, everything," he paused and glanced at her, "must be perfect, see that it is so." The king of Sparta brushed by the priestess; she bowed as he passed.

Aspasia was a slender woman with long thick dark hair hidden beneath a hooded cape. As she raised her face, the sun lit her fine features and sparkled in her dark azure eyes. Her tongue darted out and wet her full lips. She still tasted the salty sweetness of the king's skin. Her eyes feasted on his muscular body just as her lips had earlier. Her skin puckered with the memory of his rough hands grasping and kneading her breasts and her hips, pulling her toward his hunger, his need.

"As you command, Great King." Aspasia glanced up at him under her thick black lashes. Her nostrils flared and the beating pulse of her heart was visible at the base of her slender throat. Her feelings were a mixture of hate and love. Love for her king but hate that he left her each night, left to go to her, Helen, his queen.

The king left the temple, walked down the steps, and was immediately flanked by four royal guards. As the men departed two robed figures joined Aspasia.

"Have you found a suitable candidate?" Aspasia asked, watching the king's retreating back.

"Yes, he is a young prince of Ilion. He arrived here late last evening," Nephele, priestess of Aphrodite said as she dropped her hood and fluffed her long blonde hair.

Aspasia looked at her compatriot, raising an eyebrow. "A prince of Ilion? Hector is well known to me. He will not do."

"No, it is his younger brother," Polymnia, the priestess of Athena, said. She also dropped her hood, and her bright red curls caught the morning sun. "It is said King Priam cast him out when he was just a babe." With a smug smile she continued, "But he is now returned to the welcoming bosom of his royal father."

"Is he handsome?" asked Aspasia.

"She says that he is," Nephele said looking at Polymnia who smirked.

"Yes, I saw him when he was being led through the palace. He is very virile looking, but he walked about as if this were his first time out of the nursery." Polymnia giggled, covering her mouth with her hands she continued her assessment. "He ogled the serving maids and nearly ran into the prime minister."

Nephele snickered.

Aspasia rolled her eyes and shot a quick glance over her shoulder. In hushed tones she said, "Sisters, this plan has been in the making since last Eleusínios, if it is to work, we must stick together. Remember, when one of us is raised in power we all share in the glory."

"You say that sister, but I am still not convinced," Nephele hissed. "It seems to me that it will be you who will reap all the power and we will be left with what glory you toss our way."

Polymnia nodded her head in agreement. "If we use this prince of Ilion, how can you guarantee he will choose correctly?"

"He will if you play your part as I have instructed. Besides, the witch has assured me that her potion will make malleable whomever we choose. As to the other, do you forget? She was presented with an Oracle's words to set this in motion. We are just being the instruments of the gods."

"How are you going to get the potion to him? His brother and their followers are sure to be surrounding him." Nephele picked absently at her robe, her lips pursed in a smug smile.

Aspasia shook her head and sighed. "Remember, you are to be the bait sister, your charms are many and rival the goddess you serve. How difficult will it be to draw one prince away? Leave me, we must prepare for the banquet and our little contest." The priestesses lifted their hoods up over their heads, bowed each to the other, turned, and departed in three separate directions.

CHAPTER 6

The Agora

Young Paris, prince of Ilion, walked through the streets of Sparta toward the town's central marketplace, its *agora*. He and his elder brother Hector had arrived late the past evening. Their father, King Priam, being too old for the journey, had sent them to be the presence of Ilion in front of Hera, queen of the gods.

Paris squeezed between women carrying baskets, slowing his steps behind strolling soldiers, trying to keep pace with Hector who walked unperturbed at his side. Lithe young boys laughed as they weaved in and out of the *agora's* crowd, jostling Paris as they passed. A rotund woman holding two flapping chickens by their scrawny necks tried to squeeze past Paris who was bumped from behind.

"Watch where you are going!" a strange voice squawked at him. Paris glanced over his shoulder and turned ready to confront the rude person. A large white bird within an enormous, gilded cage glared back at him with huge black eyes. The bird opened its curved, black beak and stuck out a thin pink tongue and let loose a shrill screech, raised several large white crest feathers and tilted its head sideways. "Watch where you are going!" it said. Paris laughed.

"Want to purchase this rare, exceptional creature?" a merchant asked from behind the huge cage. "It is from far beyond the great waters."

"No, but it is quite beautiful."

"That it is." The merchant poked his head around the cage and grinned. "It speaks Mycenaean and Aegyptos too as well as some strange native tongue. I will include this fine gilded cage if you but purchase the bird."

"Remarkable, but I am afraid I have no desire for it," Paris glanced away from the merchant, realizing that Hector had stopped at a fruit grower's table far up ahead.

With a nod to the bird merchant, Paris quickened his steps and stopped next to Hector. A vendor, with features hidden by a hood, stepped forward and handed Paris a golden yellow apple. The young prince smiled, twirled the apple with the tips of his fingers, and hefted it. He reached into a pouch hanging from his waist, grabbing a thin piece of copper to pay for the fruit, but when he looked up the merchant was nowhere to be seen.

With a shrug he took a huge bite out of the firm, perfect fruit and the juice of the apple slipped down over his lips and chin; he wiped his mouth with the back of his hand.

Paris inhaled deeply and coughed. The acrid aromas of animal dung, unwashed bodies, smoke from cooking foods, and pungent spices caused his eyes to water. He knuckled them, blinked, and slowly scanned the *agora*.

"Hector, have you ever seen such things? Look at all these goods," Paris said, eyeing jewelers, potters, and traders of human flesh rubbing shoulders with sellers of animals and farmers showcasing their fresh produce.

"They are no more or better than those of Ilion." Hector rolled his eyes. "In fact, as soon as we have given over the guest gift and paid respect to the king and queen after the morrow's dedication and sacrifice, we should be off. I do not wish to linger here longer than is necessary."

"Look, over by that fountain, come on." He grabbed his brother's arm and dragged him toward a trader parading half naked female pleasure slaves before a gathering crowd. The core of the eaten apple slipped from his fingers and was quickly trod under foot.

Hector allowed his brother to propel him closer to the throng. "It's just a slaver, boy, what is so unusual about that?" he asked.

"Humor me, brother; I am not as worldly as you, o mighty

Hector. I was raised as a humble shepherd, remember?" Paris smiled, hiding the bitterness he still held as the cast-off son of King Priam.

Hector smirked, reached out, and ruffled his younger brother's hair.

"All right, but we have a banquet to attend, we don't want to be late."

"How can I forget, my brother, you keep reminding me?"

~*~

Athena's priestess Polymnia, along with several of her initiates, stood at the edge of the crowded market. One of the young girls had spied Paris and Hector watching the pleasure slaves. She pointed the brothers out.

Polymnia knew that men looked upon her with lust and women with envy and this was an opportune moment, the two princes were alone without the guard Nephele had been sure would have surrounded them. Since her task was to draw Hector and anyone else away from his younger brother, she dropped her hood, threw back her head, and laughed, loudly.

Hector heard the laughter and looked up, spying the priestess; he pointed her out to his brother.

"Now there is the finest piece of womanhood I have seen in quite some time. If we are to abide here for a space of time I might as well enjoy it. Come with me, I will show you how to woo a real woman." Hector clapped his brother on the shoulder and without waiting, walked off. Paris gave his departing brother a quick glance but hung back, ogling the pleasure slaves.

"Are you finding anything you desire?"

Paris turned his gaze to a raven-haired woman facing him across a vendor's table. Her ruby-stained lips curled into a smile revealing even, white teeth. Her dark-lashed eyes sparkled, and Paris felt drawn into their clear cold depths.

Hera's priestess reached out and placed a smooth hand upon his arm.

He shook his head, blinked, the woman's face swam before his eyes. He smiled. "Actually, I believe I have."

CHAPTER 7

Kallisti ~ For the Fairest

An ancient olive tree's twisted limbs spread out, casting a shadow over a sleeping Paris. He was lying curled up in the tall grass, his head cradled on his bent arm. A fly lit upon his forehead. Paris stirred and grimaced, and swiped at his face, sending the irritating insect flying off. The prince rolled onto his back. The sun was bright and hot in the crystal, clear air. Birds fluttered in the tree above him, singing in short bursts. He opened his eyes. Colors swirled and he felt the ground ripple under his body. He reached out and grabbed the grass he lay on with both hands. As bile rose burning his throat, he closed his eyes again and retched.

"Lay still, Priam of Ilion's fair son." The feminine voice echoed strangely in his ear and Paris grimaced. "Abide, the sickness will pass," she said.

"What is wrong with me?" Paris groaned.

"You are among the gods," the woman said and bent down, laying a cool hand upon his forehead. Paris cautiously opened one eye after the other. The bright sun created a swirling halo of golden light around a beautiful naked woman; in fact, she looked familiar, much like the woman from the *agora*. He smiled, it was easier this time, his stomach remained calm, but colors still swirled around him, and the ground still felt as if it moved about on its own.

"Am I on Olympus?" Paris let go the grass and tried to stand, the woman took hold of his arm and helped him up.

"You are with us, I am Hera," the woman said, and her smile was brighter than anything he had ever seen. She directed him toward a small grove of young olive trees where two other unclad women were standing. The sun created a glow around them too and Paris raised his arm to shield his eyes.

"Who are they?" he asked of the woman who called herself Hera.

"Do you not recognize Zeus' daughters, Aphrodite and Athena? Come, Priam's son, you have been chosen to be our judge." Hera drew Paris on toward the gathering. "So, sweet prince, who among us is the fairest?"

Questions filled Paris's mouth, but no words came forth. The goddesses gathered around him so close he could smell the heady musk of their bodies.

"If you choose me, I will make you mighty in battle!" the one called Athena cooed and the sunlight around her body wavered and pulsed, her red hair like an aura of flickering fire about her head. Her green eyes glowed like jewels and her skin looked smooth as marble. Paris licked his lips and staggered toward her.

"Wait, Priam's son, choose me and I will give you wealth and power beyond your dreams," the one calling herself Hera said, and Paris stopped and turned back toward her. Her dark hair swirled around her body, and she reached out a slender arm, her delicate hand caressing his cheek.

"Handsome Paris, if you but choose me, the mortal world's most beautiful woman will be yours alone."

Paris turned away from Hera and looked toward Aphrodite. Her golden hair undulated and swirled around her voluptuous body; her arms reached out toward him. He turned facing each of the women, each reaching out to him, each with an offer to garner his vote. His head spun and his stomach lurched, desire for these beautiful ladies filling his heart and body. A frown creased his forehead and his eyes watered. A single tear tracked down his cheek. Before it dropped from his chin the one calling herself Aphrodite reached out and wiped, catching it with a soft, smooth fingertip. She brought it to her lush lips and sucked, all the while holding Paris' gaze. She sighed.

"I choose you Aphrodite, you are the most beautiful of the

goddesses. Now tell me quick, who is to be my prize?"

She smiled and cupped Paris' cheek, drawing his face to within a finger's breadth, of her full glistening lips.

"She is Helen."

~*~

Helen, queen of Laconia, squinted against the glare of the sun as it sparkled on the pool of water in the center of the athletic field. She ran a hand down her thigh, smoothing the soft white fabric of her short *peplos*. The other girls, also partaking in the foot race of one *stade,* were giggling, pushing each other, but making sure not to jostle their queen.

The priest of Hermes, standing at the edge of the dirt track, cleared his throat loudly, trying to bring order to the contestants. Helen looked up, smiled, and glanced at each of the other girls in turn, silently bringing a moment of calm to chaos.

The priest lifted his arm, his hand a fist.

At the end of the *stade* the runners pulled up. Helen leaned over and put her hands on her knees. A thin sheen of perspiration covered her body, and she was breathing heavy, but still smiling.

"You allowed me to win. Shame on all of you," she laughed, stood up, and trotted over to the other young women.

"No, we didn't," Myrine, said. Helen reached out and encircled the girl's shoulders. She pressed her forehead to Myrine's.

"You cannot fool me, little one. Come," Helen released Myrine and twirled in place motioning for the others to join her. "Let us refresh ourselves, we are late for the banquet."

~*~

Hector stood in the palace's great hall, a goblet of wine in one hand and several cured olives in the other. The titian haired beauty at the agora had proved to be vapid and full of nothing but giggles and empty promises. He had quickly lost interest. Hector tossed the olives into his mouth, rolling them around, scraping the salty flesh from the pits with his teeth. He spit out the remnants and scanned the room over the rim of his goblet.

"Arturos, have you seen my brother?" Hector asked of his cousin, the captain of his personal guards.

"No, the last time I saw him he was with you, heading for the *agora*." Arturos drained his cup of imported Aegyptos beer.

Servants wove their way around ambassadors and princes, lords and ladies who milled about all gathered to pay homage to the Goddess Hera and the king who had built a magnificent temple in her honor.

"He's probably found something soft and juicy to pass his time," Hector said eyeing a plump serving girl carrying a tray of sweetmeats. She smiled as she rubbed her pert breasts against his arm, twirling just out of reach of his grabbing hand. He gave a short laugh, took a gulp of wine, turning in place, scanning the crowd once again for his brother.

"There he is," Arturos hissed grabbing Hector's arm, swinging him around so that he could see Paris walk into the great hall.

~*~

Paris rubbed his eyes as he walked from bright outdoors into the dim interior. The smells of roasting meats, spilled wine and heavy perfumes over rank sweating bodies caused his stomach to turn over.

Swirling visions of naked goddesses in an olive grove caused his head to throb, just above his eyes. His mouth was dry, and his tongue felt swollen.

"Brother, where have you been?" Hector grabbed Paris by the elbow and pushed him along, Arturos on his other side. "You're just in time for the meal, or have you already eaten?" he said with a leer and a wink. Paris remained mute, as he didn't know if the episode in the grove was real or imagined, as he had awoken cold, and alone. The three men joined the crowd as they moved toward the dining hall.

Large tables laden with platters of roast meats and

vegetables, bowls of oranges and shiny, cured olives, baskets of nuts and plates of sliced melons encircled the immense room. The crowd surged toward the tables unceremoniously scrambling onto the benches. Servants entered carrying large platters of roast meats and the seated guests grabbed at the bounty.

The three from Ilion hung back watching with gaped mouths as the high born of Mycenae and Lacedaemon pushed and shoved each other, grabbing at food and drink.

"Have you ever witnessed such as this?" Hector asked Arturos who was older and had traveled farther.

"Nay, my prince, I am as much astounded as you."

"I might be sick," Paris said staggering away from the gluttonous spectacle. Hector and Arturos let him go and walked the perimeter of the hall. Paris found a side door and pushed past servants into a courtyard open to the bright blue sky. He made his way to a wall, bent over, one hand against the warm rough stone and emptied his stomach in great heaving retches.

As Paris wiped his mouth with a back of his hand, he heard the sounds of heralds and roars of approval. Pushing off the wall the prince looked around. The approaching slap of sandals interspersed with giggles and shrill voices of young girls echoed off the stones. Not wanting to be seen, he stepped into the shadows, his back pressed against the wall. A group of smiling girls, dressed in short, athletic *peplos*, bright white in the brilliant sun, entered the courtyard. One stood out from the group, she was dressed as a young goddess Hera, her *peplos* glowed white, a belt of golden rope crisscrossed her full breasts, her cheeks were flushed, and her skin glistened. Upon her head rested a tall golden *polos* crown mimicking the one the goddess Hera wore. She was laughing and wiping her hands with a saffron-colored cloth. She stopped to return it to a comrade and spotted Paris in the shadows. Her smile disappeared for a moment as she gazed upon him. When the rest of the group also turned and spied the prince, they shrieked and pushed the young woman; she laughed and allowed them to propel her onward toward the banquet hall.

Alone again he stepped out of the shadows. The girl had

looked right at him. Her dazzling smile had made his stomach clench with desire and need. But there was something more. Something he couldn't quite place. He made his way back into the noisy hall.

~*~

On a raised dais stood King Menelaus basking in the approving shouts of the diners still grappling for meat and drink. Paris stood at the door allowing his eyes to adjust to the dim light. Menelaus was orating about his benevolence, waxing on about the beauty of the temple he had caused to be built.

The food dwindled, the servants stopped pouring wine, and sounds of discontent moved through the gathering. A catcall sliced the thick air.

"Where's Zeus's daughter, that queen of yours, Menelaus! If you won't fill our bellies or slake our thirst we need some entertainment, get her out here!" the drunk yelled, grabbing at his crotch followed by roars of approval. Menelaus read the temper of his crowd and he desired to have them envy him and his property. He stood before them puffed up with pride. With a wave of his arm he called for his most cherished possession, Helen.

Helen stepped upon the dais and whispers rippled through the room reminiscent of a wave closing in on a sandy shore. She wore a tiered skirt of deep ruby red with a loose-fitting bodice embroidered with gold thread. The neckline was cut low and revealed the curves of her young firm breasts. Her face was painted white, and her full lips tinted red to match her gown. A thin shaft of sunlight illuminated her as she stepped upon the dais. Fine strands of gold interlaced with carefully crafted golden olive leaves fell in intertwined rivulets from the crown on Helen's head. The golden tendrils covered her dark hair and glinted with fire as the sunlight caught the delicate diadem, the precious gold laying liquid over her shoulders and down her back. Her eyes were expressionless, staring off over the heads of the gathering. Menelaus reached out and grabbed his queen by the forearm, pulling her close to him. His smile turning into a lustful leer, his eyes gray hard rocks.

His lips pressed against her gold covered locks and his voice was low and menacing.

"You behave yourself, Helen," he said as he ran a hand under her bodice and cupped her bare breast. Helen stifled a gasp. "You are mine," Menelaus said his lips touching the gold of her headdress. His breath hot and moist and smelling of Aegyptos beer.

"You are my king and husband."

Menelaus released her and she turned to the crowd, a smile on her face.

"Greetings," she said with a sweep of her arm.

~*~

Paris stood at the edge of the crowd, his head aching and his mouth still filled with the bitter taste of bile. The feeling that he was back in the olive grove surrounded by goddesses washed over him in a cold wave making him shiver. His gaze centered on Helen, she had been the girl in the courtyard, and was the most beautiful woman he had ever seen, more exquisite than he could have imagined.

Aphrodite's words echoed in his head as he watched the queen of Laconia on the dais, standing close to her husband the king.

"Choose me, and the mortal world's most beautiful woman will be yours alone. She is Helen."

As Queen Helen spoke the words of welcome, her ruby lips glistened in the torchlight and his lips ached to taste her. His fingertips tingled with the imagined touch of her soft body, his breathing coming stronger as his desire for her increased.

"Brother, are you well?" Hector nudged Paris who smiled weakly unable to turn his eyes away from the woman he now thought of as his prize.

Paris's smile faded. He wiped at his lips with the back of his hand and stared at the queen.

Arturos stood on Paris' other side and looked from his prince to the queen and back at the prince again.

~*~

"My Lord King, it would be an honor for the princes of Ilion to accept your invitation," Hector said and bowed at the waist as did Paris during their audience the day after the banquet.

Menelaus smiled down on the princes as he hefted a small statue of Hera, a guest gift from King Priam. The statue was crafted of new Aegyptos gold; it was obvious to him Priam was flaunting his vast wealth in his face. Menelaus' jealousy and greed were like a hunger, the more he thought of it, the more he lusted for it. His brother Agamemnon, King of Mycenae had told him of his plan to sack Ilion, claim their wealth, and assure his status as high king over all of Lacedaemon. But with no knowledge of Ilion's legendary fortifications Agamemnon had prudently forestalled the campaign.

Menelaus licked his lips and wiped his mouth with the back of his hand, perhaps he could find another way to get that gold. A slight smile curved his fleshy lips, his daughter could be the key. Pawn Hermione off to the young one, Paris, and after the marriage he could siphon off the treasury of Ilion like wine into his empty cup, right under his brother's nose.

"Your father is too generous; he has shown me that he considers us brothers which means you both should view me as your uncle." The smile that curled the king's lips broadened but never reached his eyes. "Stay and take the evening meal with my family, your family, I wish you to meet my daughter, she will be joining us." Menelaus cradled the statue against his chest, running his hand down its gleaming length.

~*~

Paris listened without hearing the high king. His attention was riveted on the queen. Helen sat on a small, gilded throne; her gaze centered on her hands folded in her lap. He took a deep breath and closed his eyes. A vision of her wrapped within his arms danced behind his eyelids. Hector nudged him.

Shouts of challenge caused Menelaus to move away from his guests; he hugged the precious statue closer to his body before relinquishing it to the keeper of the treasury.

"Who disturbs me?" The king growled as he stepped back, sat, and leaned far out of his great chair, his knuckles white as his fingers gripped the ornately carved and gilded arms. A messenger prostrated himself before the king. "Rise and speak," Menelaus commanded.

"Oh, great King Menelaus, it is with heavy heart I must tell you of the death of your grandsire ... Catreus."

CHAPTER 8

The Bewildered and Bewitched

With the ebb tide, the royal galley sailed from Gytheio, carrying Menelaus to attend the funeral ceremonies of his grandfather Catreus. Accompanying him were three generals and his personal guard. Left behind was Helen and the forgotten sons of Priam.

~*~

"Well, that is the end of this adventure, shepherd boy, let us prepare to depart. Father will be glad to see us return." Hector was watching gulls circle and dive, their bodies white against the crisp blue sky. The feelings of unease that he felt at the agora had returned and now caused him to frown and set his jaw as he scanned the horizon.

"But why, brother?" Paris walked up behind Hector who turned to face him. "Menelaus wants us to stay, doesn't he? We are like family, yes?"

"That," Hector snorted, "that speech he made to us before all his generals and ass-kissers?" he snorted again and grabbed his brother's shoulder giving it a squeeze. "That was all show and bluster. The Great King Menelaus no more wanted us for sons than he wanted his balls to burst."

Paris snickered.

"Don't laugh, we need to leave here. This place makes my skin crawl. I for one have no love for this Sparta." Hector clapped his brother on the back. "So, tell me, why do you want to stay among these people? You would be nothing here but one more lackey of their great king, in Ilion you are son of the high king, prince among men." Hector let the question hang between them waiting for his brother's reply.

After several moments Paris turned from his brother's scrutiny and rested his palms on the ledge of the open window.

"I had a vision, or something like that." Paris waved a hand. He turned to face Hector. "It was before the banquet. I found myself among the gods." He saw his brother stiffen, his eyes narrowing into slits.

"How is that possible? You were drunk, you were—"

"No," Paris said shaking his head. "No wine or beer passed my lips. One moment I was eating a golden apple, watching the pleasure slaves in the *agora,* and the next I was lying on my back staring up at three naked goddesses."

Hector neither applauded nor denounced, so Paris wet his lips and continued his story.

"The air around me shimmered and the ground beneath me moved. They were beautiful beyond compare. And, and, they wanted me to settle an argument between them. Me, just newly crowned prince of Ilion, me, they wanted me to choose who was the fairest among them: Aphrodite, Athena, and the great Hera. How could I choose?"

"Truly, this happened? Are you sure you drank no tainted wine?" Hector knit his brows, his lips pressed into a straight line, and he crossed his arms over his chest.

"No, I mean, yes it happened, Hector, believe me. The mighty Hera helped me to my feet and there in the olive grove of Mount Olympus I chose Aphrodite to be the fairest among them!" Paris grabbed his brother's arm. "She gave me a prize. She promised me the most beautiful woman in the world, and I saw her. She is here, here in Sparta."

Hector snorted and yanked his arm from his brother's grasp. Shaking his head, he sighed.

"So, who is she, this prize?"

"Helen, queen of Sparta."

~*~

Arturos and Hector stood before the royal Ilion ship. The deep blue water sparkled in the sun and slapped against the thick wooden pilings. The smell of the Gytheio River hung thick in the air and the noise of the busy harbor echoed against the mountains at their back.

"My brother is bewitched, Arturos. We need to leave this cursed place. How soon can you get our vessel ready to depart?" Hector glanced at his cousin.

"We can be ready in two days' time."

"Make it happen, friend."

~*~

Paris sat on a low mud-brick wall in a courtyard of the great palace. He noticed not the sweet breeze that ruffled the leaves of the olive tree casting a cooling shadow. Nor did he notice the song of the birds nor the drunken flight of a colorful butterfly as it flitted between the brilliant flowers planted in unglazed pots dotting the courtyard. And the hooded figure that watched him from the shadows also went unnoticed.

The cloaked figure walked up to the pensive prince and sat next to him dropping her hood as she did.

"What ails you, prince of Ilion?"

Paris swung his head around, his eyes widened, mouth agape.

"You? How? What?" Paris sputtered and jumped to his feet.

"I am Hera's priestess. I spied you from within the palace," she said, smiling up at the prince who ran his fingers through his hair, his eyes darting up and down taking in the look of the priestess before him.

"Hera's priestess?" Paris raised an eyebrow wondering if this was a phantasm not unlike that in the olive orchard.

"Yes, my name is Aspasia." The priestess held her breath to slow the beat of her racing heart.

"But you are the woman from my vision."

Aspasia knit her brow and cocked her head to the side.

"You had a vision? Truly? Tell me of it."

The prince hesitated. The priestess carried the same visage as the goddess in the grove, but she surely was only flesh and blood. Aspasia smiled and raised her brows in encouragement. With a great shoulder-lifting sigh Paris relaxed, his brother thought him a fool; perhaps here was a believing ear for his tale. With trepidation he began to recount his adventure.

~*~

"I bow to you, prince, to have visited the August Ones on high." Aspasia had sat patiently listening to Paris tell of his episode in the olive orchard and was pleased that the witch's potion hidden within the apple had worked and he believed he had been in the presence of three goddesses.

Paris continued, "Within the banquet hall I beheld my prize sitting next to the king." He paused and Aspasia saw him look at her for the first time since starting his tale. "She is the most beautiful woman I have ever beheld. In the entire world I am sure there is no one so fair as she. I must have her and take her to Ilion as my wife." His eyes grew wide as he spoke, and Aspasia watched as his hands clenched and unclenched.

"You are speaking of our queen. Why do you think she is your prize?" The flat acrid statement hung between them. A frown creased Paris' forehead and he turned his back on Aspasia. He pursed his lips.

"How could it be anyone else?" He turned back to face her. She saw the kernel of doubt creep into the squint of his eye.

"Perhaps you are correct, perhaps not. Have you consulted a seer?"

Paris paused. "No."

"Come, let us go at once to Aphrodite's temple and consult her seer, only at that time will you be sure that Queen Helen is your true reward." Aspasia took Paris by the elbow and walked him to the courtyard's exit. "I will accompany you and introduce you to her. She is quite accomplished."

"You are most kind."

Aspasia smiled; the boy had been far too easy. Her plan was unfolding faster than she had anticipated and a diversion was necessary to slow down the pace, to wait for the messenger that was due to arrive from Aegyptos.

~*~

Aphrodite's temple stood perfect and white, shining in the bright sunlight. Blood-red roses grew on flowering bushes along the façade and pomegranate trees flanked the entrance to the courtyard in front of the temple. In the center of the courtyard was a large, rectangular reflecting pool. Floating placidly upon its still surface were two white geese.

"Abide here, my prince; I will fetch the seer," Aspasia said, directing Paris to a marble bench beneath a young myrrh tree at the courtyard's edge. She left the prince and entered the temple, returning a short time later with a young girl dressed in a long white *peplos* the hood of her cloak shading her face. Paris smiled at the slight-figured girl.

The seer looked up at the prince and his breath caught as he saw her disfigurement. The seer glanced away, and walked over to the reflecting pool. She sat on the raised edge and waved her hand over the surface. Paris walked up behind her and leaned over trying to see into the pool. The water was still but after the second pass of the seer's hand Paris thought he noticed the water begin to darken and to shimmer, as if someone had puckered their lips and blew on it. Then it was still again.

"I see our Helen." The seer continued to stare at the pool. Paris bent closer and the girl stiffened and hunched her shoulders. "I also see this prince and the two of them are embracing." The seer paused, swallowed, and waved her hand over the water.

Paris turned to Aspasia. "Do you see this too? Is it true?"

"Quiet, you will disturb her," she hissed and grabbed his arm pulling him back, away from the timid girl who might retract her promise to aid and abet.

"I sense much love, but there is also fear and anger." The seer shook her head slowly back and forth, her eyes never leaving the water's surface. "Yet, there is something else, as if the gods have a hand here. Yes, yes, I see Aphrodite, she is smiling, and she wants this prince to have our Helen, but wait." The seer looked up at Paris and Aspasia. "There is another goddess who is very unhappy. She is most powerful and will do these two harm." The girl stood with her back to Aspasia and Paris, her head bowed, her shoulders hunched. "That is all I see."

"Are you sure? Is there not more?"

"Come." Aspasia took hold of Paris' arm as he made to grab the seer. "Be at peace, sister," Aspasia said to the seer.

"And you, sister," the seer replied, averting her eyes.

"But I need to know more." Paris shook off Aspasia's hand and turned to follow the girl into Aphrodite's temple.

"Wait, leave her." Aspasia hurried after Paris and stepped in front of him.

"But," Paris sputtered, frowned, and grunted his frustration. Aspasia placed a hand on the princes' forearm.

"I believe you have your answer, prince, the gods have given you, our Helen. I know not why, but I am bound to help them. Come to Hera's temple this very evening. I will send word of the hour. Now leave me, son of Priam. I have much to do."

~*~

Helen sat before a polished round of copper. The young woman who peered back at her cast in a rosy glow had eyes a deep mahogany and hair more brown than black. The gold that had covered her dark tresses was safely cradled in a cedar box clasped against Thalia's chest. With a sniff, the old servant left her queen peering at herself.

Helen swiped at her face with a cloth, leaving a swath of bare skin beneath the white makeup. She sneered at her reflection; being placed on display by her husband always put her in a foul mood. She felt she was no more than an exotic bird in a gilded cage. A thing to be taken out and paraded before all only to garner jealousy for Menelaus as one of his possessions. How he had preened before them, soaking up their envy. Behind her an oil lamp's flame sputtered, and a servant bent to trim the smoldering wick.

Over her shoulder she said, "Leave me." She returned her gaze to her reflection, and wiped her face once more, she was sure there was a hollowness within her breast where her heart should be. She squinted at her likeness as if there was something more to be seen, something behind the beautiful woman that glared back. Her breathing rose in tempo. A whimper escaped from her lips and tears slipped from the corners of her eyes unchecked.

After her requisite attendance in the throne room, during the receiving of guest gifts, she had slipped away and walked about the palace compound. The free-flowing wine had made the guests amorous, with men taking their pleasure, as they were able; either with their equally drunk wives or the serving maids as would have them. Helen had felt too much the voyeur and with heavy heart had retreated to her rooms.

"I should rip your heart out!" she hissed at her mirror image. "You cannot love. You cannot have what others enjoy! You will forever be a Laconian, and Menelaus is your cruel fate."

With a deep shuddering sigh Helen stood. She picked up a comb and threw it. It hit the mirror dead center and bounced off clattering to the table.

A scratching came at the lintel. Helen wiped the remaining makeup from her face and the tears from her eyes.

"Come."

The cedar door swung ajar and a young girl in a blue *peplos* slipped through the narrow opening. Her eyes were averted, and her hands were clasped.

"My queen, I bring a message from the priestess of the Great Goddess Hera." The girl's voice rose in confidence as she spoke.

Helen turned at the mention of Hera.

"Yes, tell me." Helen brushed her hair back and smiled to encourage the young girl.

"It is most urgent that you come to the temple, my Lady, Aspasia, the priestess, says there has been another seeing."

"What was said?" Helen's heart beat a quick tattoo in her breast and her stomach clenched. Was it fear she felt or perhaps a small ray of hope that perhaps this time Hera would forgive her mother and herself for being a reminder of Zeus' infidelity?

"I know not," the girl said shaking her head.

"Of course. Tell your mistress I will come." The messenger bowed her head and backed out the door and the sound of her bare feet slapping the stone floor could be heard receding down the corridor.

~*~

Helen arrived at the temple and spied Aspasia in front of the giant statue of Hera. She was placing at its feet a glowing lit votive filled with olive oil, setting it next to a jar of wine and a pot of goat's milk cheese.

"Greetings, Aspasia, your servant tells me there was another prophesy?" Helen asked as she reached out a hand to raise the deeply bowing priestess.

"Yes, my queen. A dream was sent to our seer by the mighty goddess, who is ill pleased." The priestess rose and stared deeply into the queen's eyes.

"A dream of prophesies, upon the wake of my husband's leave taking. Tell me of it, Aspasia." A goddess' anger could mean anything, a death more than likely. The desire that her husband might meet his fates upon the seas and leave her free blossomed in her heart, as did the inevitable wave of guilt sending a visible shiver the length of Helen's body. She looked at the priestess, afraid that perhaps her wish could be read upon her face.

"The dream started as all visions from the goddess," Aspasia recited the tale watching the queen closely. "The seer was walking within an olive grove but this time, when the goddess appeared she was holding a shield and a bloodied sword in one hand and in the other Hera held the severed head of your husband our king and at her feet were other heads."

Helen sucked in her breath, her hand flying to her breast above her heart. Was this it, the prophesy of her freedom?

The priestess continued looking at the queen through lowered lashes, her nostrils flaring ever so slightly as she spun the tale.

"Hera's glowing gown was soaking up blood from the men at her feet writhing in pain, bathed in blood, and among them a young one, very handsome, not more than a boy. She dropped your husband's head to join the fallen and pointed a bloody finger."

"Did she speak?" Helen's voice was small, just barely above a whisper.

"That she did. She said, 'Beware a love ill begotten.'"

"Is that all? What does it mean?" Helen reached out to Aspasia but before she could touch her, she withdrew her hand and grasped her gown, her knuckles white against the vivid blue of the material. Her chin quivered and she drew a pained breath. Was her longing for love the cause of this bloody dream? She felt a deep guilt, and wished she could share her pain with this priestess. But would this woman even understand what it was like to have to play the dutiful wife, no matter how difficult Menelaus made the task?

The slap of leather sandals against the new marble floor echoed in the vast temple. Paris, with long deliberate strides came into view. He paused and spying the two women smiled and made his way towards them.

"My, my, a gathering of beautiful swans." he said, his voice loud and clear.

The two women turned, their long tresses flying about their shoulders. Paris' reference to swans made Helen draw a sharp breath and step away from Aspasia. She prepared to leave but the priestess stayed her with a soft touch of her hand.

"Abide, my lady, he means no harm, I am sure, he knows not that swans have been forbidden by your father." Aspasia turned and smiled at the prince.

"Oh, forgive me, your majesty, did I say something amiss?"

Paris asked. His eyes and smile widened. He was so enthralled with Helen's beauty and the fact of finding his prize so close within his reach that he ignored the look of shock upon her face.

Aspasia stepped around Helen and reached for Paris, brushing off the awkward silence.

"You are Paris, King Priam of Ilion's son, enter the goddess' house, and be at peace." Aspasia smiled and with an extended arm drew him closer into the circle that included the queen.

A tall, slender, white-robed figure emerged from the shadows. Aspasia's head rose and watched the Goddess Hera's seer approach.

"Aspasia, is this the seer who had the dream?" Helen asked following Aspasia's gaze.

"Why, yes."

Helen stepped away from the priestess and reached out toward the girl.

"Seer, I need to ask you about your dream."

The young woman's eyes widened, and she looked toward the priestess. Aspasia stepped in between them.

"I am afraid we must leave you but for a moment, my queen. Please, may I beg that you stay and wait for my return?" Aspasia bowed her head at Helen and Paris, turned her back and left, grabbing the seer's hand causing her to follow in her wake.

~*~

The priestess' steps quickened, as she left the temple she broke into a lope, her hair streaming out behind her, her robes bouncing to the rhythm of her gait. The seer kept up with her mistress and the two arrived at the entrance to the woman's quarters, the *gynaikonitis*, nestled deep within the palace. Both slowed their pace to a walk. With a hand like a raven's claw Aspasia grabbed the girl by the arm.

"Remember, play your role as we planned."

The seer nodded her head. Aspasia released her and walked into the cool, dim building.

The *gynaikonitis* contained a large stone floored open-air courtyard whose center held a pool of water drawn from a deep well. A large shade tree cast a cooling shadow over the sun-warmed stones. Birds sang and swooped from the branches, and some paused on the edge of the pool to share a drink with the women of the palace. A few of the women sat under the tree or next to the water. Queen Helen's private apartments fronted the courtyard and since she was away her serving ladies were at the pool laughing, gossiping, eating sweets, and drinking cups of wine.

The priestess and the seer approached, and the women stopped their conversations and stared at the interlopers. One matron stood and separated herself from the others.

"Greetings Aspasia, what brings you to us on this beauteous day?" The woman was Helen's sister Clytemnestra, wife of Menelaus' brother Agamemnon. Along with her young daughter Iphigenia, Clytemnestra had arrived on the flood tide to keep her sister company while both husbands were off to the funeral games held in honor of Catreus.

"Greetings honored lady, I have come to converse with our queen, may I request her whereabouts?" Aspasia averted her eyes as if in reverence but more to hide her lie.

"I must disappoint you, priestess, the fair Helen, is not here. But," Clytemnestra said her eyes narrowing to slits, appraising the woman in front of her. "I was under the assumption that you had bade her come to the temple."

Aspasia shook her head.

"We are here because our seer has had a dream of prophesy."

The prescribed moment had arrived; Aspasia's seer fell to the ground.

~*~

Helen stared after the retreating priestess and seer, with a quick raise of her eyebrows and a sigh she directed her attention to the prince. Her eyes softened and her lips curled into a slight smile as she recognized him. He was the boy in the shadows of the courtyard.

Paris brazenly reached for Helen's hand and grabbed her fingertips, holding them gently but firmly with his own. With a swallow he looked up from her small hand and gazed upon her face. Helen's eyes were wide, and he saw a touch of fear within them as she looked from his face to her hand and back at him again. She sniffed and tried to withdraw her fingers, but he held fast.

"Be not afraid, fairest one, I mean you no harm. In fact, you are why I am here."

"Me?" Helen squeaked out the word. She swallowed and cleared her throat. "Why me?" she asked, her voice sounding stronger.

"It was before the banquet, I was given a vision of the gods, and the beautiful Aphrodite gave me a reward." Paris wet his lips and took a deep breath. A frown creased Helen's forehead.

"A vision? Are you a seer among your people?" Helen again tried to extract her fingers from Paris' hand, but he took hold of it more firmly, grasping it with both of his hands.

"No, I am just a man, no special gifts were I given." Paris smiled.

"Will you tell me your vision?" Helen finally was able to free her hand. She took a step back and crossed her arms.

Paris smiled, raised his eyebrows once, and sighed.

"Three goddesses, two daughters of Mighty Zeus, and his queen, Hera. They stood within an olive tree grove, the smell of ambrosia filled the air as they spoke to me with voices as melodious as a summer rain and my body quivered and the ground swirled around me as I beheld them." Paris looked over Helen's head beyond the temple walls, drawing the scene back into reality once more. Helen watched his eyes dart back and forth as the prince described his vision.

"I was chosen," Paris looked at Helen, "me, newly come prince of Ilion, to choose who among those august women was the fairest. You are the most beautiful woman I have ever seen, my Helen. Just as the goddess promised." Paris reached out to cup Helen's cheek, but she turned her head and pulled back.

"Please, you are taking liberties that could be fatal for both of us."

"Fear not, we are goddess-blessed." Paris grabbed her hand and pulled her to him. He wrapped his arms about her, but she struggled, worked her palms up to his bare chest, and pushed with all her might.

"Stop this," she hissed, and Paris dropped his arms, allowing Helen to take two awkward steps backward. Once free she looked around the temple. Two young girls had entered, and their giggles echoed in the nearly empty marble columned expanse.

Helen looked back at Paris, turned, and ran, leaving the prince standing in front of the statue of Hera.

Helen quickened her steps away from the temple and back toward the palace. She felt her face start to burn, and her pulse quicken from more than her exercise. The young prince of Ilion had made physical advances toward her that she could never return no matter how handsome he was nor how much it pleased her. She bit her bottom lip trying hard to stem the smile that threatened to curl them.

~*~

"Beware people of Laconia, beware the web of deceit, the lies. Beware love ill-gotten, beware a queen's vows thrown to the wind." The seer's voice spoke the words that Aspasia had bade her to say. Her eyes were closed, and her body quivered on the ground as the women crowded around, pushing each other to get a glimpse of the god-touched person and to hear her words.

Helen arrived at the *gynaikonitis* just as the crowd was dispersing and all eyes looked right at her. She stopped and stared back; her heart fluttering afraid of what the gathering of women were thinking. Was the guilt of desire from her encounter with Paris written upon her face?

Aspasia pushed to the front and approached Helen with a

bow of respect.

"My queen, there has been another sign, my seer, she," Aspasia paused and pulled the girl around in front of her holding the young one's hand tightly. "This one, she was taken over by Hera and the goddess spoke through her."

The faces belonging to her ladies and her sister seemed to be assessing the young queen, weighing her against the words that the hapless servant had spoken. Her gaze rested briefly upon each of the women's faces as they openly stared back. After what seemed like a dozen heartbeats, her women bowed to Helen one by one, and Clytemnestra came to her side with a familial smile.

"What was the goddess' message?" Helen asked, her voice soft and hesitant.

Clytemnestra grabbed for her sister's hand.

CHAPTER 9

In the Name of Love

Helen sat staring out her chamber's window gazing down at the sparkling ribbon of the Eurotas River. No cloud marred the perfection of the deep blue of the Spartan sky. Helen wrung her hands, oblivious to the beauty before her. She sighed, rose, and paced the length of the room, her delicate leather sandals slapping the clean swept, stone floor. Bright sunlight streamed into the room, illuminating her as she walked in and out of the beams. A servant setting out her cosmetics and other toiletries turned toward her and watched as the queen fretted.

Clytemnestra stood nearby picking at her saffron-colored shift watching her sister. Helen stopped her pacing and sat before a low table, the cosmetic bottles shining in the sunlight. Dust motes danced in the beams that cloaked Helen's head and shoulders. The servant stepped up and began brushing out Helen's long, dark hair, absently running a hand down its shining length behind each sweep of the comb. Helen sighed.

"Stop acting the child," Clytemnestra said. "No one has accused you of adultery. At least, not yet."

Helen looked up at her sister waving away the servant.

"Leave us, now."

"Yes, my lady," the servant said as she bowed and made for the door. With a final glance at the sisters the woman slipped through the doorway.

"Speak freely, sister, don't hold back." Helen turned her face up toward Clytemnestra. "What is being said about me?"

Clytemnestra waved her hand at Helen. "Just the usual grumblings of jealous women; and the ravings of that drooling idiot didn't help." Clytemnestra walked up behind her sister and ran a hand down her hair, letting it come to rest on her shoulder. "That prince of Ilion is very good looking. Do you desire him, dear Cygnet?"

Helen gasped; her sister never used their mother's pet name for her, and how could she have known of her encounter with Paris; had she been seen?

"Do not call me that," she hissed, standing and walking deeper into her sleeping chamber. "I have done nothing wrong," she said over her shoulder. Helen's color rose to a deep rose pink and her eyes filled with tears. "Whether I desire a young boy or not should not be the gossip of you or my women," she said wiping at her tears.

"Are you weeping, sister? No one is going to report your night dreams to your husband. At least as long as that's all they remain."

"I have no dreams of Paris or any other." Helen's hands were clenched into tight fists. "My lot is with my husband. Father put me there and that is where I will stay." She unfolded a hand and with its back she swiped at her nose, swallowed and sniffed. "Let us not fight, Clytemnestra." She turned back to face her sister. "You are all I have. No one here cares whether I live or die. All hate me. Most of all my husband."

Clytemnestra walked the distance to her sister and draped an arm about her shoulders. "It is not so bad as that, is it little one?" She cooed and took the ball of her thumb to wipe at the tears still brimming in her sister's eyes. Helen turned into her sister's arms.

"No, I guess not. But at times the hair on the back of my neck rises as I pass by the women here at court. Their judging eyes follow me. I have no friends here. I know they whisper ill about me, as I have not given Menelaus an heir. I know they say my womb is cursed by the gods."

"If they say it, I have not heard."

A soft scratching caused both women to pause.

"Enter," Helen said and stepped away from her sister.

Hera's priestess walked into the room and dropped to one knee in front of the queen, her head bowed. When Helen did not bid her to stand, Aspasia lifted her head.

"My queen, I have come to invite you to the goddess' temple. You had wanted me to set aside a time when we might beseech the goddess together and what with the prophecies, the goddess' anger, and the king away, I thought this was most opportune. Hera *is* the goddess of childbirth." Aspasia let the sentence hang between them; she dropped her head, and held her breath, waiting to see if Helen would rise to the bait. She had come personally to invite the queen not wanting to give this most important quest to a servant.

"You tempt me, priestess. Perhaps I could also question your seer, and she can make her dream and this last prophesy clearer to me."

"Yes, and I will come too," Clytemnestra said as she stepped up next to her sister.

"The great Hera will bask in the glory of all those that worship her," Aspasia said and the cloying sweetness of her words almost made her sick. Not only did she not want Helen to question the seer, she also did not want Helen's sister. For her plan to blossom, she would have to draw Clytemnestra away. Helen alone and unwatched was her prime target.

"Sister, yes, join me." Helen reached out and took her Clytemnestra's hand in hers.

"Leave us, priestess, we will follow in your wake," Clytemnestra said to Aspasia, a slight hint of harshness in her voice.

Aspasia rose, bowed her head, and turned, leaving the women standing in a pool of sunlight.

~*~

Six-year-old Iphigeneia scratched at the door's lintel and entered her aunt's rooms unbidden.

"Momma, when are we going home?" Iphigeneia swiped at

a stray lock of deep red hair as she walked past her mother and aunt toward the open window. The young girl clawed a small hand full of raisins from a bowl sitting on a silver tray and turned back toward her kin.

"Join us, Iphigeneia, your mother and I are going to the temple to honor the goddess," Helen said and smiled at her young niece. Clytemnestra watched her daughter's progress within the room with cold, gray eyes.

"I want to beseech the goddess on behalf of my son Orestes. I was unable to bring him and worry for his safety," Clytemnestra said in an aside to Helen.

"Can we ask her about sister Electra and father too?" the young girl asked, her lower lip stuck out in a sorrowful pout.

"Yes, yes, Electra too, but your father can care for himself." Helen heard the coldness in her sister's voice.

"I did not know there was strife between you and Agamemnon." Helen addressed her sister whose mouth was a cold hard line. "Sister, why did you not tell me?"

Clytemnestra shrugged. "It is not that important," she said over her shoulder, with a brief smile.

Helen handed her niece a small honey cake from off her breakfast tray. "Come, join us at the temple. You can take an offering to the goddess and implore her to protect your sister. If your words move her, she will answer you." With a smile she pressed a small ewer of wine into her sister's waiting hands. "Perhaps, there will be good news for all of us."

~*~

Aspasia met the group at the temple entrance, she had hoped that Helen would come alone, but was sure she could draw off Clytemnestra and her daughter leaving the young queen alone and available to Paris.

"Come into the goddess' sanctuary. She will grant you succor, give you strength to face your troubles, all you need do is honor her, worship her, give her the respect and love she desires and deserves." Aspasia drew them deeper into the temple toward the most sacred site, a small private room where, as Hera's priestess, she alone communed with the goddess.

The room was illuminated by a lone polished bronze oil lamp placed at the base of a life-size statue of the goddess. The statue was painted in vibrant colors. A rich, purple woolen *peplos,* caught at one shoulder with a circular jewel-encrusted broach, was draped over the lifelike carved edifice. The statue glistened in the flicker of the flame and appeared as if it were living and breathing not carved from cold marble. Incense smoldered in large shallow bowls set on pillars flanking the statue and the heady aroma of vetiver, almonds, and honey filled the air.

Helen, Clytemnestra, and Iphigenia paused just inside the room.

"I felt that it would be better if you confronted the goddess where she was the most powerful. She has been speaking through many of late, and I fear her anger if we do not heed her warnings." Aspasia stood at Helen's shoulder and looked at the young queen.

Helen felt the warmth of the priestess' body. She took a small sliding step closer to her sister, but Aspasia moved with her, keeping a physical pressure on the queen. The priestess wanted Helen to be uncomfortable, enough to seek out someone, someone that did not play a role in the family dynamics. Someone named Paris.

But how to draw Clytemnestra and the child Iphigeneia away; the puzzle was solved for her.

"This is foolish, the goddess does not reside here," Clytemnestra said through clenched teeth. Her words came out in a low hiss.

"You are the foolish one, sister," Helen said, and her voice sounded hollow within the small marble encased room.

"Mother, I saw you with another." Iphigeneia said standing wide-eyed looking at the statue of Hera. "I saw you kiss him," she whispered, and her lip quivered. "I am afraid." Iphigeneia turned and ran out of the inner sanctuary.

"Give my regrets to the goddess, dear sister, you are the

faithful, good one of us, she will listen to you," Clytemnestra said and took hold of Helen's hand, passed her the ewer of wine, and followed in her daughter's wake.

"I had no knowledge of my sister's affair. I thought the goddess spoke through your seer of me, of my wanton desire for, for..." Helen's words caught in her throat, and she looked at Aspasia. "It was my sister who was prophesied about. My sister." Helen took a few tentative steps toward the statue of the goddess. Dropping to her knees, she put her face in her free hand and drew in a deep breath. Dropping her hand and with pain written on her face she turned her gaze upon Hera.

The flame of the oil lamp danced and steadied, casting an eerie light upon the marble carved goddess.

"Guide me, queen of Olympus, guide me along the path of my life. Fill my womb with a boy-child for my husband, for I fear for my life if I remain barren." She put her face in her hand again.

Aspasia placed a hand upon her back. It was time to move the plan along.

The priestess staggered and then spoke.

"Queen of Laconia, hear my words and be a feared." Aspasia made her voice husky and deep, all the better to mimic a goddess.

Aspasia made her eyes flicker back and forth as if watching a play unfold before her. Helen looked up; her mouth fell ajar. In shock she sat down on the cold, stone floor, her palms spread flat at her sides, her knees drawn up. Was this truly the goddess who spoke through Aspasia?

"Love ill begotten will destroy your house, only the true of heart will be spared. Blood will run, fill the sea, and great men fall. A love pure will save you, a love pure will save you all."

Aspasia collapsed to her knees in front of the queen. Helen reached out a tentative hand to comfort the priestess and felt the woman shake beneath her fingers. Aspasia lifted her head and looked into Helen's eyes to see if her ruse had worked.

"You are pure of heart, my queen. I know the goddess means for you to save your house from death."

"My heart is far from pure," Helen said looking at the floor beside Aspasia. She met the priestess's intense gaze. "She could not have meant me. I lust, I hate, and I desire to be free of my husband." Helen drew in a sharp breath. She had not meant to reveal her most secret desires. "How can she mean I am the pure one? Could it not be one of my nieces? Perhaps my daughter who I have never known, taken from me when I was just a babe myself?" Helen did not know why she bared her heart to this woman.

Aspasia shook her head.

"No, my queen, I am sure within my heart that the goddess means you. You are the pure of heart, you are the one who will find pure love."

Aspasia drew in her legs and started to rise, taking hold of Helen's hand; the two women stood together, their hands clasped. Aspasia's heart beat rapidly within her breast. Helen didn't even want Menelaus. She wanted Helen gone so that she could lay claim to the man she loved. She was sure that with the queen disgraced and out of the way Menelaus would turn to her for succor, for her strength. Thus far her plan was falling into place. Perhaps the gods wanted what she did. Wouldn't they have stopped her by now if they didn't? Or just like she had thought for some time, there were no gods, just foolish men and women believing conniving priests and priestess before her.

"Did you bring an offering for Hera?"

Helen nodded her head, handed her Clytemnestra's ewer of wine, and drew out the sweet cake concealed within her robe. She unwrapped the confection. With a sigh, she placed it in front of the statue. Aspasia placed the ewer next to the cake.

Helen licked honey from off her fingers. "It is meager, but it was all I had time to gather. I'm sure she would have preferred a sacrifice. A young lamb perhaps." Helen stepped back and looked up at the goddess one last time. She drew her shoulders up and visibly shivered. "I want to leave here. She is placing her faith in the wrong person." Helen made to walk out of the inner sanctuary. Aspasia stayed her with a hand.

"Please, my queen, I will show you the way, allow me to guide you with the hand of the goddess, she loves you and knows what lies in your heart. She makes no mistakes, forgive me if I speak so boldly."

A tight smile curled the edges of the priestess' lips and her fingers curled around the young queen's elbow to guide her from the gloom of the small chamber and out into the light of the temple.

"Of course you know Hera has shown me only contempt as I am but the bastard child of her husband. I am sure she has caused me to be barren, denying me the chance to provide an heir for my husband." Helen tried to pull away from the priestess.

"You are wrong, she does not hate you, you are but the innocent in that affair."

"That is difficult to accept. Let me leave, I want no part of goddess visions." Helen turned to walk away from Aspasia and came to an abrupt stop.

Leaning against a pillar at the edge of the main hall rested Paris, his legs crossed casually at the ankles. He examined the nails of one hand and bit at the skin of his thumb.

Aspasia's tight smile widened at the sight of Ilion's prince, now the plan could move forward.

"A guest, my queen."

Helen saw Paris, Aspasia laid a hand on the Helen's arm and felt the queen's body stiffen.

"Fear not, the goddess sends this boy to you, he is the pure love that she speaks of. Perhaps..."

"No," Helen hissed between clenched teeth. "I am no adulterer. I will not be swayed by a goddess' words." Helen yanked her arm from Aspasia's grasp and turned to face her. "No, priestess, I cannot."

"But...."

"No, I cannot." Helen turned away and made to leave. Aspasia grabbed her elbow again. She had to do something, or this moment would be lost. Ilion's prince must seduce the queen. Aspasia's heart beat wildly within her breast. It was time once more to play the goddess.

"Heed my words, beauteous Helen, child from my husband's

lustful loins." Aspasia rasped, dropping Helen's arm and standing rigid. "Heed the fate I have given you. Turn not from my blessings or worse than death faces all." Aspasia dropped her head and staggered slightly. She wet her lips and raised her eyes. The queen's eyes were narrowed.

"Priestess, do you play the oracle this day? Are these truly the words of Hera herself?"

Aspasia feared if Helen realized she was playing false her plans would crumble. But searching the young queen's face she realized that this was not the case, this girl was so naïve. Aspasia nodded her head, Helen's fingers flew to her lips, and she squeezed her eyes shut, only to open them.

Her breast rose and fell with a sigh, and she glanced at the prince still resting against the pillar, the sun streaming in from a high window, illuminating his golden hair, making it gleam and sparkle. As if he felt her gaze upon him, he turned his head and smiled, his straight white teeth sparkling.

Helen looked at Aspasia.

"I am afraid," she said and looked back at Paris.

"Yes, it is only a fool who would go forth without fear. I will be here for you as will the goddess. She will not forsake you." Once again Aspasia held her breath hoping that she had not over-played her hand.

Helen reached out and grabbed Aspasia's hand.

"Be strong for me, I fear I am far too weak to be the instrument of the gods."

Aspasia squeezed the queen's hand and gave her a smile and a nod of her head. Helen wanly smiled back and turned to face Ilion's prince. Aspasia released Helen's hand.

With a deep sigh Helen set off toward Paris. Her heart was in her throat, and she felt her palms moisten; she wiped them on her *peplos* as she neared the boy.

Paris pushed off from the pillar and placed his hands on his hips and turned his back to the approaching queen. He heard the soft steps of Laconia's queen and his heart quickened. His impatience got the better of him and he turned around catching

Helen off guard.

"Oh," she said with a quick intake of breath. She stopped and took a tentative step backwards. Her hand fluttered at her throat. She smiled. She had forgotten how utterly beautiful he was. His smile took away her breath. How was she to be a chaste wife if her heart betrayed her with the first boy that smiled at her? He was unlike the coarse male companions of her husband that leered at her while she was put on display. Those she could ignore but this one, perhaps the priest was right, and he was sent by the goddess. But could it be just to test her? She started to take another step back when Paris shot out a hand.

"Wait, don't go. I didn't mean to startle you, please, stay," he said and smiled again, his hand hovering inches from her arm.

"You didn't startle me, I had just, just, perhaps you did startle me, but you are forgiven." Helen looked down at her feet and scuffed a toe, feeling foolish and childish at the same time. She had never felt this awkward. How could this one, his eyes so empty of guile, cause her heart to skip a beat and her stomach to flutter? Perhaps the goddess did have a hand in this, just as Paris and Aspasia had said.

Paris dared to touch her arm, running the tips of his fingers down her silky, smooth skin from the crook of her elbow to the tips of her fingers where he cupped them, feeling her nails graze the palm of his hand. The muscles of his stomach clenched with desire for her.

"You are so..."

"Stop," Helen said snatching her hand away and wrapping her arms about her body. "If you say I am beautiful one more time I will leave, and you will never see me again." Her eyes sparked with anger.

"But that wasn't what I was going to say," he paused, rebuffed and looked at her, squinting one eye and pursing his lips. He shook his head. "True, you are a great beauty now, but your looks are sure to fade. Besides," he paused and craned his neck to get a closer look. "Is that a start of an ugly wart upon that nose of yours?" he said reaching as if to touch the offending blemish.

"Soon they will have to hide you away with a veil to cover your unsightliness." Paris shook his head, tsking. "There is a small hair growing from it."

Helen drew in her breath, leaned back, and her hand flew up to touch the tip of her nose.

Paris chuckled. Helen sniffed.

"You tease me," she said with a smile.

"Perhaps," Paris said reaching for her hand.

She paused and looked at the prince, here was a young, good-looking man, but she felt he was so much more. He did not take offense at her when she stopped him from complimenting her beauty. In fact, he had turned it into something that made her smile. She allowed him to take her hand and felt the warmth of his fingers as they wrapped around hers.

He was close enough for her to feel the heat of his body caress her skin; with closed eyes she inhaled. He smelled of cinnamon and green grass and the salty sea.

His voice was rich and resonated within her body, sending a thrill through her that settled low within her belly. She opened her eyes and looked at him. He had stopped talking and was smiling at her.

"Where did you go, dear Helen?" Paris asked.

She smiled again and turned her head away looking out of the temple.

"I was here, next to you," she paused, "my heart was filled with happiness, but," Helen turned back to look at Ilion's prince and a frown creased her smooth brow. "But I should not be here. I should not feel these things. I am Menelaus' wife and queen." Helen started to pull away.

"No, we are goddess-blessed, sweet Helen. Aphrodite has given us to each other. I will not turn my back on the gift of the gods."

"But why would Aphrodite want to give me anything? I keep trying to appease Hera because I know she hates me; a seer cursed my marriage in her name." She bit her lip and knit her brow. "Perhaps Aphrodite is doing this to vex Hera."

Helen searched Paris' face to see if he had even heard her words or if he was just dazzled with her beauty, as all mortal men seemed to be.

After several moments Paris' forehead creased with a frown and he tilted his head slightly. It reminded Helen of one of Menelaus' hunting dogs when her husband teased them with scraps from the table.

"How is that? Hera is a kind and fair goddess, why would she hate you?"

She smiled, sighed, and looked at him with something akin to humor.

"I am Zeus' daughter. You see," she paused and turned her back to him, to hide her shame, "he changed himself into a swan and seduced my mother. I am the product of his lust and my mother's adultery."

"Oh, yes, I had heard of that. But," Paris paused and took her hand, turned her around then gently brought it to his lips. "Doesn't that make you a goddess too?" he asked looking at her over her fingers.

Helen shook her head and allowed Paris to kiss her fingers, feeling his soft lips as they caressed the back of her hand. He turned her hand over and brushed his lips across her palm.

"I am as mortal as you," she said with a sharp intake of breath.

Paris drew Helen closer to him and when they were just a fingers-breadth apart he wrapped his arms around her waist.

"I am mad for you. You are my prize; I must have you."

His breath was hot against Helen's cheek. Instead of his words causing her fear they made her want him, madly, just as he said. Her belly tightened and her heart beat a strange rhythm beneath her breasts. Her legs wobbled and a weakness came over her, if Paris were to release her, she was sure she would fall.

Was this what her women giggled about, gossiped about behind their hands, their heads drawn together in private conversation? They had conversations that Helen rarely listened to but was keenly aware of.

But was this love?

Paris used a single finger to tilt Helen's face up to meet his. His lips gently brushing hers, his breath hot against her mouth.

"Love me, sweet Helen."

The temptation to melt into his arms and give herself over to her body's longing was strong. The longer she stood there with his hot breath tingling her skin, the more difficult it became to step away.

Paris' lips touched her chin; she felt the tip of his tongue on her throat at the spot that beat her heart's rhythm. Her breath came fast, and she closed her eyes not wanting him to stop. His hand released her hand and it dropped to her waist, then her thigh and grabbed at the fabric of her *peplos*, groping for an opening.

Every scrape of his fingertips against her thigh caused her belly to ripple with feelings she had never known. She wanted him to find her flesh, she wanted his fingers to touch her and when they did, she drew in her breath and her eyes flew open. Paris lifted his head and covered her open mouth with his, thrusting his tongue between her lips, tasting her.

Paris' seeking fingers cupped her buttocks, and he drew her close to his body, pressing her against him. Helen felt the hardness of his need and knew she should stop him, but she could not, because she wanted him, wanted his hands on her body and his hardness deep within her belly more than anything she had ever wanted before.

"You are mine, sweet, beautiful Helen, you are mine." Paris' hot breath scorched her cheek, and his lips burned her skin.

"What is this?" A woman's sharp voice cut through the fog that clouded Helen's heart and she recognized it.

Her sister Clytemnestra ran up to the couple and pulled Helen out of Paris' arms.

"You fool, what are you doing?" Clytemnestra hissed at her sister, yanking her around to face her, looking into her sisters' lust filled eyes.

"She has been given me by the goddess, you can not interfere," Paris said as he wiped his mouth with the back of his hand and made to take Helen's arm.

"She is queen of Laconia and Menelaus is her husband, she is no more yours than I am!" Clytemnestra pushed Paris in the chest with her free hand and quick-stepped her sister out of the temple. Helen glanced back at Paris.

Paris followed the women out of the temple toward the palace. He was met at the gate of the women's quarters by several armed guards.

"Stay away from her, she is not yours and never will be. Be gone!" Clytemnestra growled deep within her throat, her teeth clenched and her eyes flashed anger. She slammed the gate in his face.

~*~

"What kind of a fool are you?"

"No more fool than you, dear sister." Helen was peering out her window at Hera's temple. She turned to look at Clytemnestra. "Didn't your daughter accuse you of adultery? Did you not take to your bed someone other than your husband? What did Agamemnon say? Does he know?"

"Stop."

"No, I will not stop. You have no power over me sister. I will be with whomever I wish to be with. Besides," Helen stopped and turned back to the window. "Besides, he loves me, and I love him."

"Love, what do you know of love? You are still a child."

"We are goddess-blessed."

"Goddess-blessed, what nonsense is that?" Clytemnestra walked up behind Helen and turned her around. They stood nose-to-nose; so close that Helen could smell her sister's perfume and the aroma of oranges on her breath.

"Paris had a vision, and the goddess Aphrodite gave me to him."

"You are more of a fool than I thought. Dear Cygnet, he is playing you. He is a minor son of a king, and he wants to make a prize of the wife of King Menelaus, brother of the great High King

Agamemnon. Don't you see? Goddess-blessed, it is just a ruse."

"No, it is true," Helen whimpered. "And don't call me Cygnet."

"But don't you see, you are the daughter of mighty Zeus, Aphrodite would never just give you to some nobody prince. If that were even true."

"It is true," Helen said looking down at her toes peeking out from the edge of her gown.

"We will see about that. I've set guards on your door."

"You can't do that! I am queen here, not you!" Helen stood up to her sister.

"Don't be an imbecile. Because of your imprudence you could lose Laconia. I will not allow that to happen."

Not waiting for a rebuttal, Clytemnestra turned away from Helen and left her standing in the middle of her rooms.

~*~

The sun rose and set, and Helen chaffed under the watchful eyes of her sister and several of her women. Guards stationed outside her door barred the way each time she tried to leave. Never before had she felt so caged, so chained to a life that she was unhappy in. At least Menelaus was absent, which left her body free of his brutal nocturnal assaults. But when he returned, would Clytemnestra or one of her women tell him of her infidelity? And what would he do to her when he found out? A feeling of panic bloomed deep within her breast. Her breath caught in her throat, and she flung herself onto her bed, burying her face in the pillows to muffle the sound of her cries.

~*~

"This is taking too long; Paris and his brother will be leaving on tomorrow morning's outgoing tide. Your plan, Aspasia, has fallen flat. Our dear queen has not fallen into his arms like you said she would." Polymnia, Athena's Priestess, stabbed a finger at Aspasia, her lip curled and eyes half-lidded with disdain.

"Patience, sister, there is another part to this plan." Aspasia flashed a quick, tight smile. "I have foreseen this problem and have taken measures," she said with a sniff.

"Oh, another potion?" Polymnia sneered. "One that will turn our queen's heart toward adultery?"

From her robe Aspasia withdrew a square fold of papyrus tied with a leather thong.

"This is the document that seals our queen's fate." Aspasia held aloft the square, placed it carefully down in front of her fellow conspirators, and smirked.

"I read not the scratches of diplomats, sister. Reveal their meaning." Polymnia pushed the papyrus back toward Aspasia.

"I can read them." Nephele, Aphrodite's Priestess, snatched the papyrus up, untied it, unfolded it, and scanned the writings, using a slender finger to mark her progress. "Very good, sister, you have sold our queen to the Aegyptos king! They believe Menelaus has divorced her. They are ready to receive her and her household as soon as the seas are favorable for travel. My, my sister you have outdone yourself. Now just how are you going to get our queen aboard a galley heading to Aegyptos?" Nephele threw the papyrus at her sister priestess' feet. Aspasia retrieved the precious document, looking up at her fellow conspirator.

"You have but little faith in me. I have also enlisted the help of the Priest of Hermes. When I revealed that Hera spoke through me and also added it to our seer's prophesies, well, he is appalled that our queen would betray our high king and wishes to help us rid Laconia of her, seeing how she is half Aegyptos."

"So, the rumors are true," Polymnia grabbed Aspasia's arm and turned the priestess to face her. "So, that means that...."

"Yes, sister, Queen Leda was Aegyptos. In fact, she was Pharaoh's sister." Aspasia pried Polymnia's fingers from her arm.

"What about Ilion's prince? He still believes Aphrodite gave Helen to him," Nephele's words came out in a sneer.

"Do you not find the prince comely enough? Do you not want to walk in Helen's very sandals? He will be very easy to sway, much like before. As to the crone's potion, yes, I have a bit, enough to cloud his mind again and make him believe anything you tell him. Hear me out sisters, we will be rid of that cow Helen at the next filling of the moon."

~*~

Myrine set a tray of fruit and cheese and warm, fresh baked bread in front of a morose Helen sitting on a stool before an open window, her arms crossed. The girl poured a cup of wine, setting the ewer next to the tray.

"Can I get you anything else, my lady? Do you want your lady sister, perhaps?"

Helen waved Myrine away shaking her head and looked out of the window toward the shining new temple that rose high on the hill above the palace. She was not hungry, though she knew she should be. And she certainly did not want her sister nearby with her disapproving looks.

She toyed with her food, pushing several olives around the tray, picking up a piece of bread, shredding it bit by bit only to toss the crumbs at a dove that perched on a branch of an olive tree just outside her room.

She raised the cup to her nose and breathed deep of the retsina wine only to scrunch up her face at the aroma of pine needles and put it back on the tray. Rising, she paced her room taking her gown within her hands and bunching the soft fabric between her fingers.

She couldn't clear the vision of handsome Paris from behind her eyes. Every time she closed them, his smile and his sparkling eyes were there. She felt he was mocking her. Yet all she wanted to do was let him touch her, let him run his hands along her arms and her body. She felt her heart beat behind her breasts, a tattoo of longing, of need, which was so very foreign to her.

She threw herself on her bed and drew the fine woven blanket up over her shoulders, burying her face in the pillows. She wished to sleep, to forget these feelings, but sleep filled with forgetfulness would not come.

As nightfall neared, silent servants entered. One took her untouched food tray away and another lit several oil lamps before leaving. Helen heard the muffled voices of the soldiers she knew still stood guard outside her door. How long would her sister keep her sequestered within these rooms? She guessed that she would be released only when Paris left for Ilion.

Helen watched the flame of a lamp flicker and dance and wished she had never met him. Now she knew what she missed most from her union with Menelaus—love and desire. She rolled onto her back and tears welled up in her eyes and rolled down her temples soaking into the pillows. She swiped at her eyes and sat up. Anger at the gods, anger at her parents, anger at Menelaus filled her body and she grabbed a pillow and tossed it across the room. The act did not ease her temper, only made her feel more impotent as the pillow bounced off the wall and unto the floor.

She rose from her bed. She wished to leave her rooms, longed to feel her feet carrying her toward Hera's temple. The moon was full and round, just rising into the sky, and the stars sparkled like a frosting of salt crystals scattered by the gods.

Lying back on her bed, she listened as the palace grew quiet and watched the light from the oil lamps in her room gutter, leaving her alone in the dark.

She started to nod off but was roused when the sound of raised voices and retreating steps in the corridor gave her hope that perhaps she had been left unguarded. Rising, she went to the door, her slender fingers pried it open, and she peered out. Lit oil lamps hanging from the ceiling cast deep shadows up and down the empty corridor. She held her breath and opened the door just wide enough so that she could slip through. She stayed to the shadows and her bare feet made little sound as she raced out of the palace; free at last.

Arriving at the temple, she ran up the steps and into the vast main columned hall, the clean white marble glowing in the moonlight. She shivered and realized how foolish it was of her to come here. The night had grown cold, and she had no *himation* to cover her, and Paris was nowhere in sight. But that didn't stop her,

her feet carried her deeper into the temple toward the tiny inner room where she knew the statue of the goddess Hera stood strong and silent in the dark.

Helen left the inner room's door ajar, and a shaft of moonlight knifed into the small sanctuary. She crept inside and stood in front of the goddess' statue. Looking upon the serene carved face, she wished she had oracle sight and could hear the goddess' voice. She wanted to ask why Hera had shown her what love was like now that she could not have it. Was that the curse? To finally awaken the need within her heart only to have it cruelly ripped away.

She shivered and wrapped her arms about her body. Standing in the moon lit room she looked about and saw a lone oil lamp and a striking stone next to it. Kneeling, she pulled on the wick, breaking off the charred end; she wiped her fingers on her shift and took up the stone.

It took several strikes, but the wick caught from the sparks, a small halo of light blossomed in the dark and the oil-fueled flame glowed blue tipped with yellow.

Helen sat down at the foot of the goddess and buried her face in her hands. She looked up at the statue towering overhead.

"Why? Why did you not leave me ignorant of these feelings? I could have gone my whole life without knowing the pain of love, the hurt of wanting someone I cannot have. Why? Do you truly hate me so much?" She reached out a hand and touched the cold marble carved robe under the drape of the purple *himation* clothing the statue.

Helen dropped her hand; she felt so tired. She curled up and rested her head on her arms, and with a huge shoulder-lifting sigh she closed her eyes.

~*~

The door to the inner sanctuary stood ajar and the slight glow of the oil lamp flickered and danced on the wall. Paris had not returned to his brother but had been waiting outside the temple unable to do anything but dream of his prize. He was surprised to see Helen run across the outer temple toward the sanctuary and with renewed hope he followed her. He paused at the door and listened to her beseech the goddess.

Paris stepped into the room and walked over to where she lay. He wanted to take her into his arms and soothe the pain he had heard in her voice. Before, he just wanted her as his due, his gift from the goddess Aphrodite, but now after hearing the pain in her voice he felt she was more than that, more than just a beautiful woman to bed and parade in front of his peers. A frown creased his brow and he knelt beside her, placing a hand on her head, caressing her hair, feeling the soft texture against his palm.

Helen gasped, sat up, and turned to face him; her eyes wide.

"You frightened me," she said even as recognition curled her lips into a smile.

"I am truly sorry, my love. I saw you enter and almost left you alone, but when you lay down at the foot of the goddess, I was afraid something was amiss, so I, well, I didn't mean to frighten you." Paris returned the smile and offered Helen his hand. She took it and he helped her to her feet and drew her into his arms, kissing her gently on the lips.

She made to step out of Paris' embrace, but he held her fast.

"Please, I can't be seen with you. I am still queen and Menelaus' wife. My sister would...," her voice trailed off, not wanting to put words to her fear.

"He does not deserve you, come away with me. My brothers and I sail on the next tide. You will be welcome in Ilion; you can be my wife. I will—"

"No, I cannot. My life is here, here in Sparta. Menelaus would never just let you take me. He would come after me and—"

"But you love me, I know you do, I heard you pray to the goddess. Come with me. I will love you and protect you."

"You are so kind and gentle, but—"

"You do love me," Paris said, his lips so close to hers.

"Yes," she replied, her voice just a whisper. Taking her fully into his arms, Paris kissed her deeply. She wrapped her arms around him and pressed her body against his.

"You are mine and I am yours," he said lifting her up into his arms.

Helen stopped worrying about her life as queen and wife and sister and listened to Paris' heartbeat deep within his broad chest. She closed her eyes and let him take her where he would, his arms firmly holding her safe and warm. She buried her face against his chest and smelled the dust that clung to his robe, and the tang of his sweat was sweet to her nose. What if he did bring her to Ilion, what is the worst that could happen to her? If no one saw them leave, no one would know where she had gone. Perhaps they would not know it was Paris, perhaps it would be some time before Menelaus returned to Sparta and it would be too late; she would be gone.

Paris carried her over to the corner of the small room. He set her on her feet while he took off his short *himation* and laid it on the floor. He stood before her, hesitant.

"I love you, my sweet, beautiful goddess."

He knelt next to her, and she put her finger to his lips to silence him.

"Love me."

Paris cupped Helen's cheek within the palm of his hand, lowered his head, and kissed her lips, gently tasting her. He lowered himself beside her and ran a hand from her cheek to her breast, slipping her gown from off her shoulder. Helen's breath quickened as his lips and tongue nibbled and tasted the tender skin of her neck.

"You are so beautiful, I want you so much," Paris said against her shoulder. He licked her skin and Helen arched her back, pressing herself against his mouth. She wished he would stop his words and just take her in his arms, and not stop until he had taken everything from her that he wanted. She wanted him on her; she wanted him in her. She ached with a need she had never felt before.

With her hands she grabbed his head and directed him to

her breast, pressing him to her. She closed her eyes and gasped as he suckled her.

Paris' hands pushed away her gown until she lay beneath him naked. He let go of her breast and trailed kisses down her stomach, and with every touch of his lips her legs spread wider allowing him entrance, allowing him to take her, love her. He raised himself up and looked down at her.

"You are mine."

As he entered her, she knew that her life here as Menelaus' wife and queen was through. She wrapped her arms around him and arched her back, pressing herself against him. With every powerful thrust he tore away the ties that bound her to Laconia.

Paris cried out as he released his seed within her and she felt her own pleasure build, a feeling her women had told her about, but she had little hope of ever feeling herself, until it broke over her body in a giant cascading wave.

CHAPTER 10

A Breath of Air is Nephele

Helen slipped back into her rooms before first light. The oil lamps in the corridors were guttered and she heard the first stirring of servants and guards. Quickly she closed herself behind the cedar door and ran her hand over her body. She could still feel Paris's hand upon her, still feel his lips on her lips, still feel him deeply inside her. A shiver ran the length of her body, and she pushed off the door. The ship to Ilion would leave on the next tide, which left little time for her to plan her escape.

~*~

"Shepherd boy, where have you been all night? We leave when the tide turns." Hector threw a leather pack at his body servant and turned toward his brother, his arms akimbo, his legs planted wide.

Arturos and two sailors carrying a large chest crabbed past the princes.

"Ah, he came back," Arturos said. "Take that to the ship and come back for the others," he said over his shoulder to the sailors.

"I want to bring someone with us." Paris pushed past his brother and into the cabin grabbing robes and sandals throwing them into an open chest at the foot of his bunk.

"And who would that someone be?" Hector followed his brother with Arturos bringing up the rear.

"Helen." He didn't look at his brother, almost afraid of the response he was sure to get.

"Helen, you mean Menelaus' queen? Are you mad?" Arturos made to push past his cousin to reach Paris, but Hector stopped him.

Paris threw a sandal into the chest and whirled around.

"The goddess gave her to me; besides, we love each other!"

"Love? What do you know about love, shepherd boy? Have you bed her yet?"

Paris turned his back on his brother and slammed the chest closed.

"That must mean you have not. Bed her, your love will leave as soon as your lust is slaked."

"Listen to your brother, Paris, bed her and let us leave this cursed place before the king returns to run you through for making a cuckold of him!"

"Neither of you understand; Helen was given to me by the gods! She is coming with me no matter what you say."

"Where are you off to?" Hector grabbed his brother's arm as Paris walked past him.

"I'm going to make an offering to the gods for our safe passage home."

Hector looked askance at his brother. "What you need is find yourself a *hetaera*." He grabbed his crotch. "Just stay away from temples, goddesses and especially Laconian queens."

"That is a splendid idea," Arturos said as he left the two princes alone.

Paris pressed his lips together and blew through his nose.

"When you are done come to the ship. I don't want us to spend any more time in this place than we must." Hector turned his back on his brother running his fingers through his hair.

"I know that is how you feel, brother, you need not worry, I'll be there. When does the tide change?"

Hector looked out a window at the sky and marked the position of the sun.

"When the sun is high in the sky, don't be late, shepherd boy," he said over his shoulder.

~*~

Paris did not heed his brother's suggestion of finding a pleasure slave, instead he found himself at Aphrodite's temple. He laid an offering of sweet cakes at the base of the goddess' statue within the courtyard. He didn't hear the sound of delicate sandals upon the raked path. Nor did he smell the sweet perfume of roses and honey from the smooth skin of the priestess as she walked up behind him.

"Thank you for your kind offerings."

Paris was startled by the words and jumped up, turned around and upset a clay carafe of wine next to the cakes. Upon the carafe was a small painted scene of a man holding a young lady's hand, standing within an olive grove. The carafe broke and the wine ran before the statue of the Goddess soaking the sweet cakes turning them red.

"Who are you?"

"I am Aphrodite's priestess," the woman said.

Paris looked her up and down noting her long golden hair that curled down over her shoulders and arms. Paris looked deep into her large, hazel eyes; he was sure that he had seen her before.

"You are a guest of the king and queen," she said, wetting her full lips with the tip of her tongue.

"Yes, I am Alexandros-Paris, but you may call me Paris. My father is the king of Ilion."

"Yes, I know who you are."

"You do? How do you know me? Are you a seer as well as a priestess?" Paris paused, blinked, and squinted his eyes. "Tell me, how does one so beautiful become a goddess's priestess? Are you chosen at birth?" Paris smiled, the corners of his eyes crinkled and a dimple in each cheek deepened.

Nephele returned his smile. "You ask too many questions, handsome Paris."

Nephele felt herself growing warm and her stomach fluttered as she watched the prince standing before her. This was a task that she was going to enjoy. She held out a shallow bowl of olives that had been laced with the remaining witch's potion and offered Paris to partake of them. He smiled and gathered several into the palm of his hand and popped one into his mouth, his teeth scraping the salty flesh from the pit.

"Forgive me, you are on your way to see Queen Helen, yes?" Her cool hand rested upon his arm, and she lightly scratched her nail along his skin. Paris watched the progress of her finger and raised his gaze back up to her face. He smiled. He put another olive into his mouth. He looked out of the temple's courtyard toward the palace.

"Oh, yes, but, I, ah, have sometime before my, uh, audience." Paris blinked. He felt the ground swell beneath his feet, and he was at once light-headed. He reached out for the priestess and took her by the elbow. Paris leaned into her, and she carefully steered him toward a small marble bench beneath a blooming apple tree. "You have not told me your name." The prince blinked several times. The priestess smiled and her teeth sparkled in the sunlight.

"No, I have not." She flipped her golden hair with a delicate, slender hand. "My mother named me Nephele, but my father had wanted to call me Helen. You have my father's gentle manner, so you may also call me Helen."

The scent of the blossoms and the buzz of bees mixed with the aroma of the Nephele-Helen's perfume. Paris closed his eyes and inhaled deeply.

"You are mine now, sweet prince. Aphrodite gave you to me and me to you. Do you see that now? Do you see that I am the one who is your true prize?"

Paris opened his eyes and Nephele-Helen was bathed in an aura of light just like when he was surrounded by the goddesses in the olive grove.

"You are my prize?" He paused and searched her face and saw how beautiful she was. The most beautiful woman he had ever beheld. "How could I have been so blind? Of course, you are." Paris reached for Nephele-Helen, drew her to him, and kissed her. Her lips tasted of wine and the sweetest fruit he had ever eaten. Her skin was silken beneath his fingers. He buried his face in her soft hair and inhaled, the aroma of lavender and linen filled his head, and he felt himself grow hard with desire of her.

"Take me, my Prince, I am the one that is yours."

CHAPTER 11

Love is but a Lie

The sun was tracking its way across the sky. Its bright rays moved deeper into Helen's bedchamber, and slowly began to fade. She sat in a chair in front of a window and waited for Paris, her chest packed for the voyage. His last words to her had been to wait and he would come for her. Dread filled her as the hours passed and no Paris.

A sound of low voices in the outer chamber reached her ears and she rose and walked expectantly toward her door.

A scratching on the lintel made her jump.

"Come." Her heart fluttered within her breast.

The door opened and a tall, dark man entered and bowed his head. He was dressed as an acolyte and a medallion hanging from a chain about his neck proclaimed he was of the god Hermes.

The acolyte slowly raised his head. His eyes were the color of a cold, cloudy sky. A chill ran down her back. She returned the acolyte's naked stare. He neither blinked, nor turned his eyes away. A flush of anger passed over her; it was maddening to be made to feel uncomfortable in her own rooms.

"My lady, I am Dorius. It is time, you are to come with me."

"Did the prince send you?"

"I am to escort you to the ship. Do not be afraid, my queen; you will be safe with me."

"I asked you a question, Dorius. Did Alexandros-Paris, prince of Ilion send you?" She wanted to believe that Paris was behind this man; she wanted to believe Paris really loved her and wanted her just as he said.

"I am an acolyte of Hermes. The god's priest sent me, and I

am bound to obey my master, to keep you safe."

A chill again ran the length of her body. Should she go? Did she have a choice? She was sure that if she stayed here in Laconia that upon his return Menelaus would find out about her unfaithfulness.

Dorius turned and opened her chamber door. "Please my lady, we will be late. The ship is due to depart, and you must be aboard."

~*~

At the port on the Gytheio River, Hector and Arturos stood at the rail of the ship waiting for Paris.

"We can't leave without him."

"Why not? He has chosen his bed; let him lie with that cow! Menelaus will put him out of our misery when he returns, the fool." Arturos looked at Hector and shook his head. "Are you sure he is your brother?"

"There he is now. And it looks like the queen has agreed to accompany him. Make haste and get underway as soon as they come aboard." Hector pushed off from the rail.

Paris boarded the boat, his hand firmly holding the Priestess Helen's hand pulling her along behind him.

"Brother, we are here and ready to depart!" Paris said flashing a large smile at the men.

Hector and Arturos stared at Paris looking from him to the priestess.

"Who is this? This isn't the queen," Arturos said shaking his head. He threw up his hands and walked off.

"I thought you were bringing disaster down upon our house, but this isn't Menelaus' queen." Hector clapped his brother on the back.

"No, I was mistaken, Aphrodite gave me one of her own, this is the Goddess' priestess, and she too is named Helen." Paris said drawing her up next to him, taking her hands in both of his and kissing them, staring deep into her eyes. Helen smiled at

Paris, turned her gaze to his brother, and dipped her head in his direction.

"Fine, I don't care who you take with us just as long as we leave this place. Cast off, Captain, we sail for Ilion!" Hector yelled, leaving his brother standing in the middle of the ship's deck his arm around his prize.

~*~

Two figures swathed in dark cloaks stood head-to-head within the recesses of Hera's temple. Their whispers hissed in the shadows.

"The deed is done."

"Have you the proof for the king?"

"The girl will swear to the queen's disgrace."

"Good."

"What of the rest?"

"You will be rewarded when I get mine."

Footsteps echoed against the marble walls and the two figures dispersed and melted into the long shadows of the dark corridor.

~*~

"Lady Clytemnestra," Aspasia bowed her head.

"What do you want?" Helen's sister took in the demeanor of the priestess and felt something was amiss. "The queen is not here."

"That is why I am here. It seems that my queen has left with her lover."

Clytemnestra's eyes widened and she took two quick steps toward Aspasia, grabbing her by the arms.

"What did you say?"

"Your sister, our Queen Helen, has taken a lover. Now it seems she has run off with him." Aspasia spoke slowly, her eyes never leaving those of Clytemnestra. Helen's sister dropped Aspasia's arms and turned from her, one hand covering her mouth, her other arm hugging her body.

"Was it that prince of Ilion? Paris?"

"Yes."

CHAPTER 12

He Returns

The sun rose hot and white, no clouds marred the brilliant expanse of sky and the calescent air hung heavy on everyone's shoulders as the days neared the dance of the *Hora Capo*.

A young initiate raced into Hera's temple, her bare feet slapping against the night-cooled stone floor. She pushed open the Phoenician cedar door that led to the goddess' inner sanctuary.

"Menelaus has returned," the girl gasped out between huge gulps, her slim chest heaving.

~*~

"You stinking, filthy *hetaera*, do you know what you have done?" Menelaus took hold of Aspasia by the throat and closed his fingers, his lips pulled back from clenched teeth, his eyes hard slits of rage. The priestess' hands flew up and clawed at his fingers trying to pry them loose. Her eyes were wide, and she gasped for breath. "I should kill you! You brought this bastard into my home and let him take my wife, the daughter of Zeus!" He shook her hard, and opened his hands, pushing her away. Aspasia landed on her back and gulped in lungsful of air. She sat up and rubbed her throat, tears sprang to her eyes.

"Yes, the goddess knew exactly what she did. She rid you of a barren wife," Aspasia paused and swiped at her eyes, "and proved her a traitor."

"What? Hera did this? Do you play me a fool?" Menelaus unsheathed his short sword and pointed the tip at her breast. "Quickly bitch, explain."

Aspasia pushed the tip of the sword away and took a deep breath. Her heart beat rapidly and she felt light-headed with fear.

The words came tumbling out of her mouth. "Hera spoke through her seer; Aphrodite spoke thus too. It was the prophecy. The crone told you that if you wed the *hetaera* Helen, she would bring destruction and death to Sparta, and it has come true."

"Liar."

"If you want that cow, go get her!" Aspasia spit on the floor of the temple, lay back, and covered her face with her hands.

"You've made me a laughingstock." The king pitched his sword. It hit the floor with a clatter. He threw his head back and a deep roar escaped his throat. "I'll kill her," he yelled.

Aspasia had not expected him to act like this. She was sure that he had wanted to be rid of Helen. How could she have been so wrong? Menelaus turned to leave; she knew she had but one chance.

"Hera, Aphrodite, and Hermes have a plan."

He stopped, his back to her. Menelaus rubbed his chin and walked back to Aspasia. He grabbed her by the arm and yanked her to a standing position, pulling her close. They were nose to nose.

"What plan?"

"She saw you with Ilion's princes, she saw the look in your eyes when you beheld her golden statue." Aspasia swallowed. Menelaus's eyes narrowed and he licked his lips, but he did not stop her. Aspasia saw that she had been correct; Menelaus wanted Priam's treasure. She pushed what she thought was her advantage. "You want Priam's wealth. Hera has given you the perfect excuse. She knew you would want revenge; she knew you would want to kill Priam's son for stealing what was yours. You do want revenge." She reached up and stroked his cheek hoping his anger would subside and he would see the wisdom of her plan. "And I want you."

Menelaus snorted. "So, you want to be my queen." He was so close to her she could feel his growing lust. Aspasia pressed her body against him.

"Yes, I would make a much better consort." The priestess

licked his throat, tasting the saltiness of his skin. Menelaus grounded his hips against her, and Aspasia gasped. "I can give you a son, an heir, she couldn't, but I can."

The king growled and covered her lips with his, thrusting his tongue inside her mouth. He fumbled with the priestesses' robes, ripping them down from her shoulders, laying bare her breasts. He backed her up against the nearest wall and hiked up her skirt shoving a finger inside her, feeling her wet and ready for him. Aspasia reached under his kilt and grabbed him, drawing him to her. He thrust inside her, not with love, but with anger and lust. Aspasia's back scraped against the stone wall, and she felt the warmth of her blood.

The priestess ripped her mouth away from the king and cried out in pain. Menelaus reached up, grabbed her by the throat with one hand, closing his fingers around her neck. With each thrust he squeezed feeling her small bones beneath his fingers. Her eyes were wide with fear, and she whimpered. Clawing at his hand she squirmed beneath his body. His free hand covered her mouth and nose. She raised her chin trying to escape his grip, her eyes wide and filling with tears. Menelaus uncovered her nose and mouth and grabbed her throat with both hands, his thumbs under her upturned chin. Aspasia gulped in air, and he covered her open mouth with his lips kissing her deep and slow. He broke off the kiss and stared at her. With a quick jerk he snapped her neck.

Aspasia's eyes closed, her hands fell away, and she grew limp. With the last beat of her heart Menelaus poured his seed inside her with a roar escaping from between his grimacing lips.

Menelaus let Aspasia's dead body slump to the floor. He stepped away from her and turned his back, adjusting his clothing. Bending down picking up his discarded sword he stepped out of the sanctuary and with long strides exited the temple.

"Guards!" Menelaus yelled gesturing to several of his personal followers waiting for him.

"That Prince of Ilion has murdered Aspasia our priestess of Hera and stolen my Queen Helen."

CHAPTER 13

Helen ~ Obedient to the Voices of the Gods

Helpless is what I was before the combined power of the goddesses—Aphrodite, Hera and Athena. As I was led aboard the merchant galley, I believed I heard their laughter mixed with the cries of gulls winging drunkenly in the sky.

When I asked if Paris would follow in another ship, silence was all the answer that Dorius would give.

How could I have been so blind to trust Paris? Was his love a lie? Was everything he told me a lie? Tears welled up in my eyes.

When my parents had chosen Menelaus from the hundreds that had sought my hand, as a wedding gift a seer had scryed my fortune. I had not thought of it these many years. The crone's words echoed now within my breaking heart.

"The folly of jealousy and vanity will
rip you from love's arms,..."

The breeze off the dark cobalt-blue sea wrapped around my body, holding me in place on the pitching deck, carrying me toward an unknown destiny.

END OF PART ONE

ABOUT THE AUTHOR

Debra J Giuffrida

Debra Giuffrida describes herself as a Renaissance Woman or just a Jill-of-All-Trades.
She currently is trying her hand as a writer having enjoyed careers as a banker, graphic artist, wine steward, chef, and groom for hunter/jumpers and pleasure horses.
Her love of Ancient Greece and Egypt was sparked at a young age when she was gifted a copy of Lucile Morrison's book the Lost Queen of Egypt and a small replica of the famous bust of Nefertiti.
She was born in New Jersey but grew up in the Central Valley of California. She currently resides in Northwest Arkanses.

Made in the USA
Las Vegas, NV
24 July 2024

92866807R00066